Hob Hurst's House

I0658457

Ophelia Finsen

Also by Ophelia Finsen:

Lovers of Old Films
This is Living
Society of Lost Causes
The Women of Jimanac
Skye
The Romanian
At the Upper Villa Tyde
Perception
You Stole My Thunder
Bella Donna
George

For my Father,
who loved walking in the North Yorkshire Moors.

"Ma! Ma!"

Little Mary Longbottom raced down the hill, summer sunlight shimmering through her childish curls. She bounded over grassy hummocks, dodging half hidden stones and tree roots: all mapped local knowledge of an outdoors childhood. Her cheeks were bright red with the exertion, her breathing giddy with excitement. She was moving so fast she might have grown wings and flown to the bottom of the valley. If only she could, for to impart the news even more quickly.

Ann Longbottom, more frequently referred to plainly as Ma by a multitude of demanding young mouths, barely gave the background noise a second thought as she kneaded bread against the heavy kitchen table. There was always something, and it was rarely a day that Mary didn't come home with some tale or story of nonsense.

She looked up, sweat beading on her temple as Mary alighted in the kitchen doorway. Her bonnet had come off, saved only by the long ribbons Ann had added and carefully knotted. This attention came from the experience of lost clothes they could ill afford. What now? A pretty butterfly? Hidden birds' eggs in the knot of an old tree? It was all magical, but with six children and a house to run, she didn't have time in the day to stop and think on these small wonders of a child's world.

"They're moving in!" Mary announced.

The toddler, Gilly, playing with a broken spinning top, looked up and giggled at her sister.

"Who's this? The sparrows? Maybe the frogs?"

"Up at Pines Lodge."

Ann stopped in her work, her attention now properly caught. "They're moving into the old Cornforth's place?" It had stood empty for almost a year, up for sale for the repayments of debts.

Mary clapped her hands in glee. "An old hob is moving into Pines Lodge."

Ann lobbed the bread dough roughly onto the table. "Don't talk nonsense, girl. You know hobs don't move into good folks' homes."

Mary grinned at her. "This one is."

Ellen Withers paused a few steps from the front door of her new home, her arms full of linen. What a place to be brought to. On top of the hills, remote and far away from civilised folk. A long way from home, and all that was familiar. People spoke in an odd way around here, and they didn't like strangers. Just look at that woman puffing her way up the hill towards them. Not even moved in proper and already the locals were coming to gawk at the outsiders. She didn't know why she'd taken this job.

She decided to take a moment's rest from carrying the family's property, and watch the local woman approach. Short and stocky, even disguised by all the undergarments and padding, Ellen guessed those hips had pushed out more than their fair share of children already. A bright red face, coloured partly from exertion, partly from the hard work, the weather and a general lack of care. Tatty messy hair, of a lank blonde shade. The woman's colouring gave the added effect of looking as though she had no eyebrows. Not what you'd call a beauty, but Ellen didn't suppose people could be fussy round here.

In her own turn Ann Longbottom regarded the young lass at the Cornforth's old home, making assumptions and drawing conclusions from the girl's appearance. She could not yet be twenty, no children, just a foolish young thing. The girl wore a bonnet which covered most of her hair, but even at a distance Ann could see that what hair showed had been carefully arranged. The wind whipped down over the tops of the moors, sweeping through the girl's skirts. Those were not the clothes of farming folk. Although she didn't look that rich. There was a certain way she stood, almost territorial with one hand on her hip and a smirk on her face as she watched Ann hurry up the hill. Was this to be the new mistress? She looked like she could be trouble.

Ellen nodded to Ann as she strode up onto level ground and approached the house. She held back as a couple of men carried a bulky piece of furniture into the building. "Good Morning," Ann said to the newcomer. "One of my children said she saw folk moving into Cornforth's place. I didn't believe it, but here you are."

Ellen cocked an eyebrow. "Cornforth's place, like?"

"Well, it's not Cornforth's anymore..." Ann stumbled over her words. The Cornforths had lived here for generations, sheep farmers and a family that were a much a part of the dale as the earth itself. But a few bad years, a disease through the flock, family deaths and a father that had built up debts before dying last winter trying to cross the moor in a drunken haze had left Amos Cornforth with no alternative but to sell up. It wasn't these folks' fault that the Cornforth family history came to such a miserable end of circumstance, but Ann couldn't help but feel a little hostile. It was a good stone house, with barn and outhouses. The villagers had heard about the asking price and the trouble Amos Cornforth had experienced selling. The debtors wanted their money. The price had been dropped. These newcomers had purchased themselves a tidy little bargain.

"Aye, that would be right," Ellen confirmed, not offering any details.

The two women, one only seventeen, the other twenty nine but with the look of a forty year old, eyed one another up. The newcomer had a very distinct accent, further north than round here. Perhaps Durham.

"Well, I'll welcome you to Colmondale," Ann offered.

Ellen nodded. "I'd never heard of Commondale till two weeks ago, when he told me we were off to live at this god forsaken place."

Ann reddened at the sound of the bastardised version of her home village name. "Colmondale," she corrected.

Ellen either misheard or didn't care. She simply nodded and repeated her error. "Commondale."

"Are you the mistress?" Ann started, watching as the men were now carrying a heavy wood chest embellished with fancy ironworking. These were folks of a different breeding to the locals. "What I mean to say, what do you go by?"

Ellen simply snorted.

There was a light cough, and a woman appeared in the shadows of the doorway. She hung back, uncertain of what she ought to do, before almost physically dragging herself into the sunlight. If it hadn't been for her dress, Ann would have taken her for the maid from her demeanour and the general air about her. This one did not have an inflated opinion of herself. But she was indeed the mistress, although she could have barely been any older than the Durham girl. She was in a dress of mustard colour with three quarter sleeves and lace flowing from the cuffs. She had rich dark hair that was tied up off her face. No bonnet. No stays in the dress at present either, for the woman was heavily pregnant, and judging by the size of the expanse, Ann wondered if it might even be twins. The woman breathed in and turned to look at Ellen. From the new angle Ann could see there was some old damage to the woman's face. Damaging to what was otherwise a strikingly pretty face. Her upper lip seemed pushed out from the base of her nose on one side. What Ann didn't know was that this was the result of a harrowing tooth extraction three years ago. In trying to pull out the left upper canine that was believed to be causing pain at the time, the blacksmith had wretched too hard and snapped the woman's front jaw bone. It hadn't been set properly and had healed with this protruding bulge. The offending tooth was still in place and hadn't caused a day's pain since.

"Ellen, could you please take the linen inside?"

Ellen glared into the middle distance, feeling her nostrils expand in irritation. There was a moment when it looked as though she might not do what her mistress asked, before she swung around the pregnant woman without looking directly at her. She disappeared into the building.

Ann was a little lost for words. This woman dressed like the mistress, but was meekly observing the ground as if she didn't dare meet the eye of a farmer's wife. "Apologies, I didn't hear who was moving in," she started. "That I mean to say is we'd not heard which family..."

"It is the Hursts," a man's voice interrupted.

For a moment Ann thought the very air had spoken, until the man stepped fully out of the doorway, and out of the shelter of his wife's skirts. He gave Ann a shock, and she did her best to hide her horror. She could see why little Mary might have come running down the hill claiming a goblin was moving into the farmstead. He was not a tall man, in fact a couple of inches shorter than his wife. He had a lithe, slim body that was almost boyish, and yet his head was that of a mature man, and the size of a tall man at that, with a well defined jaw and a shadow of stubble that grew furiously upon his face. A beaked nose and twinkling sharp eyes completed the picture. It was not a pleasing arrangement. His long hair was tied back at the base of his skull, and on top sat a black hat. He was dressed in dark blue jacket, waistcoat and trousers, with well made black boots, and carried a knobbled and highly polished walking stick in one hand. This one was not shy and retiring, rather he would boldly look wherever he pleased. Calculating, almost reading the very thoughts in her head.

Ann glanced from man to wife. Why, there must be at least twenty years between the two. How on earth had such an ugly specimen caught such a pretty girl?

He abruptly broke out into a sharp grin at Ann, and took his hat off to perform a little bow. "Hobart Hurst esquire at your service, madam," he introduced himself. His accent was not local or particularly northern. Ann couldn't place it, only that it didn't match Ellen's at all. "And this is my good lady, Mrs Hurst."

"Maud," the woman whispered when Ann caught her eye.

Hobart watched the local woman closely, guessing she was the main gossip sent up to gather information for all the other hags down in the valley. "I am a merchant," he told her. "A purveyor of goods, both fine and essential. I have good links with London and the trade coming in at Whitby, Redcar, Saltburn and so forth. I transport the goods to the burgeoning towns, the fine manor houses and the good families that are used to a certain standard of living. Certainly if the people of Colmondale need any supplies, they are only to ask. I will of course be making regular trips here to check up on my little family."

Ann was still watching Maud. Despite the sheltered life she had lived, merely with the duties of children and housework, having never travelled more than twenty miles from the place she was born, she could tell that this was a very odd marriage indeed.

Hobart tapped his stick on the ground, a little irritated by the two silent women. "I don't believe I caught your name, madam."

"Mrs Longbottom," she said, quickly remembering her manners. She looked at Maud again, catching her eye this time. "Ann," she said quietly. Then more loudly and to all. "We Longbottoms live in the bottom of the valley, close to the Cleveland Inn. If you should ever need anything, please just call."

"We may need use of your local knowledge," Mr Hurst said. "We will be in need of some domestic help, only part time and not live in. There is only Ellen Withers and this is a busy property to manage."

"Only while I am incapacitated," Maud added, gesturing towards her expansive belly. "Particularly on wash day, we could do with an extra pair of hands."

Ann nodded. This she would keep for herself, for her own family could do with some extra money. Either she or Elizabeth Mary would be up. She noted that there was yet another strange accent. Maud was clearly a Yorkshire woman, but certainly not from round here. She sounded like the West Ridings. What an odd collection of incomers, all outsiders, both to the folk of Colmondale and each other. "Not a problem, leave it with me," she said. "A woman in your condition needs to rest up. Your first child, madam?"

"Children!" Mr Hurst answered loudly on behalf of his wife. "I've seen more than two feet pressing out many a night." He burst out into laughter when he saw the horrified look on Ann Longbottom's face. Clearly that wasn't something men were expected to talk about around these parts. Be damned with these straight laced narrow minded little folk. "And now you must excuse us," he continued, taking a telling tight grip on his wife's elbow. "There is much to be arranged and my wife needs her rest."

Ann nodded, feeling this to be the oddest of introductions she had ever endured. What on earth did it mean for the village?

Even at twenty-eight Amos Cornforth had been too weary of life to hold any ill feeling. Through no fault of his own, he had found himself selling off the entirety of family property upon his father's death to clear the debts his father had amassed. Amos had few ambitions, but he wished to be considered fair and good and wished to treat alike all those owed, tradesmen and friends and relatives who had unwittingly lent money. Not a single farthing was reduced from any bill, not that Amos would have had it any other way. When the task was complete he had nothing more than the clothes on his back and his good name.

The family had been sheep farmers for generations, eking out a tough life for themselves on the moors. Amos had been courting a local girl in the next village and they had expected to marry shortly. That had fallen through along with everything else when his father died and the truth came out, horrifying and embarrassing piece at a time. Amos could never have supported a wife, with no money nor home, so it was probably just as well that she had abruptly severed all contact. She put some distance between herself and the little hamlet of Colmondale, and was soon engaged to a tradesman away over the hills in Helmsley.

Amos had simply had no idea what to do with himself once the debts were paid. All he knew was farming, and all he knew was the local area. Distant relatives could barely support themselves and offers of help were few. The locals agreed that he could take on the ruined hovel at the opposite end of the village. No one could remember who owned the one room, roofless ruin, but agreed no one particularly wanted it, and if Amos Cornforth could fix it up; it could be a place to live.

The old family land still needed managing and the flock tending. The new owner of Pines Lodge, a Mr Hobart Hurst, was a merchant and had no interest in tilling the land. So it came to pass that Amos returned to the work he had always done, but for a meagre wage and a draughty home at the end of the day. It had been a relief to have this much familiar in his life after the prospect of having to turn to vagrancy or worse.

In the autumn the Hurst household had increased when Maud Hurst's babies were born, two twin girls, identical in appearance, but as opposite ends of a magnet in personality. Even as babes and toddlers it was clear that they were going to lead very different lives. Eleanor, the eldest of the girls, was a dreamer and a wanderer. Even when she learned to crawl and could barely go more than a few metres, she would soon disappear out of sight. She was a curious child, and quite thoughtless. She would wander without a care for the weather, time or distance, and would be found in unexpected places, all the time further away from the family home as the years passed by and her legs grew stronger. Gillian, the younger, was a prim and proper little girl, already in full receipt of her manners without having to be told. Her mamma never had to ask 'where is Gillian?', for she always knew, and Gillian was always in sight. Always doing her chores, saying her prayers and playing nicely with the other children.

Hobart Hurst had not been in the valley when the girls were born, and in fact it was a good four weeks before he first set eyes on the twins. Although he was pleasant with the children, he had no great interest in them, nor his property, and trusted his land manager, Amos Cornforth, to deal with all rural issues, bringing in an annual profit for the small estate. He was a canny trader, and was often in one of the ports along the Yorkshire coastline, arranging transportation, making deals, and always calculating the profit line. He was a great walker, and could cover several miles quickly. He got to know the moors like the back of his hand, hiring a local guide for the first few months after his arrival. He had the poor lad marching up and down the moors, back and forth from village to village, different routes criss crossing one another until the poor lad didn't know in which direction he was supposed to be leading his patron. When Hobart Hurst was content he could cope alone, he dispensed with the lad's services and set to business. He was seen scuttling across the moors at odd times of the days and year, when bad weather or a dark night would have put other people off travelling, Hobart Hurst would be seen walking down into the valley with a sack of goods upon his back. Sometimes he had a donkey with him, but it seemed that he preferred to move quickly and alone.

Despite the miles he covered, the heather scratching at his clothes and in wet weather the mud splashing up his legs, he was always shod in the most impressive set of footwear. Quality boots were something he came to be known by. Mr Hurst could certainly arrange for footwear to be sent to a client. But no person's shoes ever lasted as well as those worn by Hobart Hurst. The mysterious cobbler who was creating such boots, that man of magical fingers, was one of the few things Hobart Hurst chose to keep a complete secret and nothing would compel him to share the name. It was surprising for such a cunning trader, who could have certainly set up a lucrative partnership with such a cobbler. But it was never to be.

They were an odd family, Amos reflected as he stalked over the moorland back towards the village. Any outsider moving in was talked about and viewed with suspicion for a long time. But it was usually only one outside at a time. With the Hursts, it had been three, and usurpers at that, taking over the Cornforth's place. People had shook their heads, saying it wasn't right, forgetting the fact that they had promptly called in their debts as much as the next man and knew Amos had been left with no other choice. And now almost six years had passed and people had grown accustomed to the strangers. The maid from Durham, the mistress of the house from a little West Yorkshire village called Haworth, and the master from Derbyshire, although no one had ever gotten the exact location from him. Not even the magistrate when stopping by for one of their drinking sessions, had pulled the full history of Hobart Hurst from his tongue, only getting him to admit that he hailed from somewhere in the Bakewell region.

His thoughts were interrupted as he heard light and childish singing coming across the heather. Foolish travellers, traders and drovers passing by, had sometimes heard this singing and mistaken it for the little folk, but Amos knew this voice too well to think there was anything other worldly about it. He changed his route, glancing up at the sky as he went. It would rain this evening and this little lady ought not to be out in the moors much longer.

He found Eleanor Hurst curled up in a dip, nestled down in a fortress of purple flowering heather. She was playing with a feather she had picked up at some point, and was singing to herself, oblivious to the outside world. Amos tipped his cap to her, a pointless gesture because she was still unaware that he loomed over her.

"Afternoon Miss Eleanor,"

The girl looked up at him and smiled.

"I think your mother will be worrying where you are."

She shook her head. "I'm all right."

"Aye, for now you might be. But you shouldn't be roaming the moors as much as you do. The hobgoblins will have you if you don't watch it."

The child looked at him, a little unimpressed by the suggestion. On any other child he would have assumed the look meant she didn't believe a word, only then Eleanor advised him that she'd already met the local goblins, and they'd informed her that she had nothing to fear from them. Amos laughed, not unkindly. "In that case, you'll have met the hob on the hill, won't you?" he crouched down and pointed away to the north from where they were. "You see that slight rise in the heather there?"

"Yes."

"Hob on the hill. That's where he lives."

"No he doesn't," Eleanor retorted. "He only goes to that hill to play his fiddle."

Amos burst out laughing. This one always did have a canny way of looking at things. "Come on, you'll need to be away home in time for your tea."

The girl yawned and flopped back into the heather. "I'm tired. I think I'll stay here for the night."

"I don't think so," he said, pulling her up onto her feet. "I'll walk you down."

"But I'm tired," she complained, stamping her foot to the dry, peaty earth before looking up at him and breaking into a grin. "Will you not carry me?"

"I've had a long day working."

"But it's so high on your shoulders."

It was only a mile to the house and Amos was a soft touch when it came to the Hurst twins. In fairness Gillian never asked a thing, but he was sure he would have done anything she wanted, had she only asked. They were a sweet pair of girls, as pretty looking as their mother. He bent down to let Eleanor scramble up onto his shoulders, and then they were away down the valley towards his old home, Eleanor whooping with delight.

When they reached the family house Ellen Withers, the maid, was coming out of the door. She had a wicker basket over one arm and a very fine embroidered shawl about her shoulders. As she turned her back to them to shut the door, Eleanor's eyebrows went up and she whispered to Amos that it was Mamma's shawl the maid was wearing.

Ellen turned back and jumped as the figure of Amos Cornforth was suddenly in the farm yard. She nodded curtly at him. "Mr Cornforth."

"Miss Withers," he said. "Looks like you've picked up the wrong shawl by mistake."

She snorted and gave him a withering stare before setting off down the hill into the village.

Eleanor pulled at his ear.

"Ow! What was that for?"

"She's always taking Mamma's things."

"It's a wonder your parents still employ that woman."

"She does sew nice dolls though."

The front door opened and Maud Hurst stepped out. She looked tired and drawn. Taking a deep breath she stretched her back as she put her hands to the back of her hips. She stopped whatever she had thought to do when she saw she was not alone. "Mr Cornforth."

"Mrs Hurst. I believe I found something of yours on the moors."

"Eleanor Hurst, what have I told you about roaming those moors? You will get lost."

"Mamma, I've brought you a feather."

Amos lent to the side to slip the child off his shoulders and around into his arms. He stepped up to the mistress of the house to pass her the five year old. As the transaction of wriggling child was made from adult to adult, Maud accidentally grasped at

17

Amos' forearm. It was sinew and sun baked skin. She held back a gasp and quickly let go, covering her embarrassment by fussing over her child. "Thank you, Mr Cornforth."

"My pleasure." He doffed his cap to her, not sure of what more to say but wishing he could stay. "I'd best be getting back to the village."

"Yes, of course. I hope this didn't waste too much time."

He smiled at Eleanor before leaving. "Not a waste of time."

Indeed it was a strange set up, he mused to himself as he followed Ellen Wither's tracks down to the village. Hobart Hurst was a very lucky man indeed, and yet he was absent from his home for much of the time. Even when he was there he seemed to scuttle in the background as though he didn't quite belong. He didn't appreciate what he had. Maud Hurst clearly had all the material comforts a woman might want, he was sure she was a neglected woman.

Hobart Hurst was never what one could call a traditional or archetype husband by any stretch of the imagination. Sometimes he could be particularly kind, such as a month or so later when he first learned that Maud was now carrying his child. The evening she told him coincided with his return with a little velvet pouch for her. Although he never really explained how he had come by it – and it was probably best for all that its true history wasn't revealed – inside there was a piece of medieval Spanish jewellery, that one of his contacts had come by and brought back to Saltburn for a trade. It was a piece of distinct workmanship, in gold with blue set stones hanging from finely crafted golden hinges. They were alone in the master chamber that night, with only a couple of flickering candles to provide light in the room. Maud was already in her shift, with her hair untied and flowing down her back. He pushed aside her hair with a knobbled hand and put the necklace around her neck.

"Every mistress of the house ought to have at least one fine piece of jewellery," he had told her.

Maud looked back at her reflection in the tiny looking glass. Illuminated by candlelight. And if she put her face at just the right angle, the damage to her front upper jaw was hidden in the shadows, and she could pretend she was a beautiful woman. Not a woman, but a real lady, with this set of jewels about her neck.

It was one of those times when Hobart showed her a kindness. There were many, although none could ever compare with the first kindness he had shown her six years ago when he had suggested they marry. And she supposed she would have to be forever grateful for that, and take the rough with the smooth.

For although Hobart Hurst could be capable of acts of great kindness, there were also times when he could be very cruel indeed.

Ellen Withers, now in her early twenties, hummed to herself as she waltzed in solitude around the main room of the house. It was the place where the family ate and received guests. It was all very la-de-da, but then the Hursts were much better off than most of the farming folk round these parts. And they got visitors who expected a little more than sitting in the kitchen with a tankard of grog. There were other merchants, traders, magistrates; and then of course the shifty looking types, smugglers she guessed, who would turn up in the dead of night wanting a quiet word with the master.

She paused in her dance and tilted her head just so, held out her hand to view herself in the little mirror she'd brought with her from Durham. The Spanish jewels, barely a month in the house, looked very fine around her neck. Maud didn't know Ellen had them just now, but she wasn't stupid enough not to notice that Ellen took liberties with her possessions. She never said anything, for mistress though she might be according to the marriage licence, Ellen liked to think that Maud knew her place. Just now she was resting up in the bedroom and the twins were asleep together. Mr Hurst had departed for Whitby two days ago, so that left Ellen with the run of the house.

She smiled at herself, and twisted so as to catch the light in the jewels. They looked very fine on her, certainly a lot better than that donkey-kicked-faced woman Hurst had chosen to marry. Maud didn't usually wear the necklace, instead it was kept in a little wooden box she had by her bedside. It was only right that Ellen knew where everything was. One couldn't help but notice when one kept a tidy house.

Taking off her mop cap and untying her hair, she danced around the table, imagining she was a fine lady that all the men lusted after. So busy she was in her fantasies and self-admiration that she neither heard the door open nor close. It was as she was spinning back up the side of the table that she felt that uncomfortable sensation of being watched. She came to a graceless stop only a moment or two from colliding into her master.

Hobart Hurst stood as a stone carving, any emotion pressed down inside save for the stern look on his face. His eyes flicked from Ellen's face to the necklace she wore. She opened her mouth to say something, wanting to tell him about Maud, and more importantly about herself, but she couldn't quite find the words.

Soundlessly Hurst turned from her and went to the master bedroom.

Maud had been asleep, and was only just coming out from her doze. This pregnancy was taking it out of her, and she was only four months gone. She was quite sure that this time there was only one child in her belly, and yet this seemed to crave more of her than the first two combined. All she wanted to do was sleep.

The door opened, casting light into the room. She sat up, feeling groggy and still caught in a dream state. She could see her husband's silhouette in the doorway, and wondered if she were dreaming. He had only left two days ago and had not intended to be back for at least three weeks. She could not possibly have been asleep that long.

She swung her legs over the side of the bed. "Husband, I..."

There was no opportunity to say anymore. Hobart rushed up to her and slapped her hard around the side of the face. Maud cried out in surprise, consciousness swelling upon her suddenly as she clasped her stinging cheek. He had never hit her before; she simply couldn't understand why this was.

He grabbed a handful of her loose hair and dragged her from the bed, flinging her on to the floor. Ignoring her shrieks, he grasped his walking stick and thrashed her over the back as she scrabbled on all fours to try and get away from him. Maud was terrified. She didn't know what she had done to warrant this. She had heard of other women being beaten by their men, sometimes for a reason, sometimes simply because they were drunk. Hurst had been full of alcohol before now, but she couldn't smell a drop on him tonight. She tried to get out of range of his kicks and hits, her vision blurring up from the tears that poured. Her nose filled with mucus and it became harder to breathe. She tried to keep herself in a curled form, to protect the unborn child.

Out in the kitchen, Ellen sat down in a chair by the fire and listened to the husband beating his wife. Sometimes, she thought to herself, it was the only way, especially with a woman like Maud. In having no respect for her own position, she showed disrespect for him. Ellen took off the necklace and carefully slipped it into the black velvet bag. It would probably be best to antagonise him no further this evening by wearing it anymore.

In the bedroom Hurst moved up behind his wife and put a leg on either side of her hips to pincer her into a stationary position. He grabbed her hair again to pull the sobbing fool up onto her knees. Hunching over, he put his mouth close to her ear. "The maid is wearing your jewels."

Maud felt her stomach knot. Ellen Withers. She had been trouble from the first day. They had never met before she and Hurst had gone to hire the girl, and she wasn't from the same area as Maud, so she couldn't have known the story. And yet she seemed to have a natural understanding, and took great joy in the misfortune of others. She had taken liberties ever since they had come here. Maud knew she was no lady and hadn't been able to discipline her.

Hurst shook her roughly when he got no reply. "You behave as though you are a disgrace."

She could sense he was winding up to punch her. "Please!" She shrieked, "for the sake of our child."

The punch never came and instead he threw her across the floor. "Get out of my house!" he roared. "Go sleep in the barn. I do not wish to set eyes on you again."

Barely managing to get to her feet, Maud fled from the room, picking up her shawl that Ellen had discarded on the way to the main door. She left the warmth of the kitchen and stumbled out into the dark night. The wind howled through her, blowing her hair across her face. She felt the baby move to kick her in its own show of disgust. She ran over the yard and wretched open the barn door, flinging herself into the hay and disturbing the mice with her sobbing. She had faced some difficult times, and yet had not felt quite as desolate as she did now. It had been uncovered and pointed out to her, what a pathetic excuse for a lady and a gentleman's wife she was.

Ellen Withers smiled to herself as she watched Hobart Hurst come out of the bedroom and slam the main door shut. Good riddance, she thought. Maud Hurst was a spineless, simpering thing, and certainly not suitable to be the wife of a merchant. She supposed if she were ever going to take her opportunity, now would be the time. "I do believe I have done you a great favour, Mr Hurst."

He flashed her a dark stare.

"I always knew she was no better than me. She's no lady. In fact I'll warrant to say she was a kitchen maid before she came here," she continued boldly. "What happened, did she get you trapped with that pregnancy, and blackmailed into marriage? I don't think you have to stay with such a woman. I think there are better candidates for the position of Mistress Hurst."

Ellen didn't really know how it happened, for he could move quickly when he wished. He was suddenly over her and in one fluid movement raised his stick and whacked her face with the knobbled end. The force threw her out of the chair and onto the flagstones, one of her teeth skittering across into the darkness. Ellen felt blood in her mouth. She twisted around to stare up at him.

Hobart Hurst was furious. A vein throbbed on his temple. "You disrespect me. And you disrespect my wife."

Ellen sneered at the mention. "You should throw her out for good. I'd take her place."

He hit her again with the stick. Ellen tried to hold back the pain, but she could feel her cheek starting to swell.

"I would not touch a low born tramp such as you."

"She's no more high born than I am."

He hit her again.

Ellen pulled herself onto her feet and moved out of range of his stick. She turned to face him. Perhaps she had misjudged this situation. Whatever the hold, he wasn't going to abandon his Maud that easily. He probably already knew everything that she had guessed about her. "You know, don't you? What she really is?" She would have to drive her nails deeper. "I'll tell them; I'll tell everyone in the village. They won't have anything to do with her."

Hobart's fury exploded. He rushed across, grabbing her by the back of the neck and slamming her body down across the table. "You'll do no such thing."

The shock of the collision with the sturdy wooden table winded her for a moment. Then the sobs came up from deep inside her chest. She couldn't help herself. Ellen Withers didn't like anyone to get the better of her, but it was beginning to look as though she was not to win this battle. "I'll leave you," she sobbed. "Then you'll miss me. You won't get anyone else to this god forsaken place."

"And where will you go? Back to where I found you?"

"I'll go back north, back to Durham."

He leaned over her as if to bite her neck. "After what you did?"

Her sobs tumbled over in the back of her throat. She was abruptly quiet. She'd gone to Hurst with good references, albeit written before the incident, before anyone knew. She'd left that place before it could catch up with her. But of course, Hurst travelled a lot with his business. The gossip would have caught up with him.

"It's all gossip and lies," she said feebly.

Hobart grinned. "And what about what you said to Tommy?"

Ellen felt cold.

"That last night..."

She stared in horror across the table. "No one could know about that."

"Ah, but that's where you're wrong," he hissed. "I know everything. Even when I'm not here I live in the shadows. I see and I hear."

"No."

"You will learn some respect you disgraceful wretch!" he roared, his anger bubbling up against out of seething threats. Ellen squeezed her eyes shut as he raised his stick, but he only threw it across the room to go clattering by the far wall. He let go of her neck and Ellen dared to open her eyes, to start to breath and to believe the worse was over.

"You will not leave this place." Hurst stood by the fire. "You will serve my wife and you will behave."

Ellen started to scream as he stepped away from the fire with a metal poker in his hand. She struggled against the table, trying to get up and run away, but the little man moved too quickly. With a sharp thwack, following by a piercing scream, he brought the metal rod down against the back of her ankle. As she fell back against the table, he hit her other leg, before falling into a rhythm of battering the maid's legs, refusing to stop until he had heard that satisfying noise of cracked bone.

In a dark side room two little girls huddled together under the bedclothes and clutched to one another for dear life. They did not dare to make a sound for fear the wrath would come howling to them. Little Eleanor's nightdress was soaked in tears. Gillian kept her eyes tightly closed and worked her way through the Lord's Prayer again and again, hoping and praying that the Lord would see fit to keep them both safe that night.

Ann Longbottom was still watching Maud Hurst cautiously despite the fact they had already worked for a good five hours. Maud was determined to pick up the slack, and wouldn't let the fact that she was pregnant stop her doing anything. The bruises on her face had filtered through to an ugly yellow, helped on by a poultice brought up from the village by the old woman Marsden the morning after that dreadful night. A week ago. She had just known without having to be called, and had turned up shortly after Hobart Hurst had departed. She had gone straight to Maud's aid, but had hung back from so much as looking at the maid until the lady of the house said Ellen could receive medical aid. Somehow Old Marsden just knew these things, she always had. She had a way with the herbs and the healing, and had helped many a family over the years, for there was no doctor living in the village. Not that many could have afforded such professional help.

Today was wash day, and Maud had essentially taken over the maid's role. Ann was up helping more than usual, as there was a lot to deal with. Not only was there a household to run, but farm business was busy. The sheep had been sheared, and although Mr Hurst had arranged for much of the wool to be sold, a certain amount was kept back for the family, for carding, spinning and then either for knitting or weaving later in the year. With the money the Hursts had, Ann didn't know why they just didn't hire a new maid, or why in fact the family home was situated where it was. Why was a merchant's family not living in one of the towns? There was a lot about the Hursts she didn't understand.

Maud had been surprisingly open and vocal about all that had happened, and during that first week Ann had been taken aback by just how much the woman had divulged. She guessed she must have been lonely, having no kin in the area and abandoned by her husband most of the time. That and being stuck in a home with a disrespectful and arrogant maid, it can't have been an easy few years for it. Perhaps it was a relief to actual speak of these things, and to be heard.

Ellen Withers was a mere shade of what she had been. As the light had just started to tumble down into the dale, Hobart Hurst had opened the barn door and informed his wife that what happened with Ellen was her choice. He had disciplined the wretch, but he cared neither way if she chose to fire the girl and throw her out of the home. Quite frankly, he did not care if she died of her injuries and the cold walking across the moors trying to get home. And with those words, he had left with no hint as to when he might return.

There had never really been a choice in Maud's mind. She had kept the girl on. Ann thought she was a soft touch, after the years of insult, and now to keep a maid who would be an invalid for a couple of months. From what Old Marsden had mentioned, the backs of the girl's ankles were shattered, and although she had set and bound the bones with herb dressings, Ellen Withers would never walk properly again. When the bones eventually did heal she always walked with a halting gait, and those pretty slim ankles she had been so proud of were now deformed fat swollen sausages. But somewhere in this, the simple act of mercy, without any expectation of gratitude, finally won Maud the respect and loyalty that any mistress ought to have taken as her automatic right.

The children were all down in the dale at Ann's home, being looked after by her eldest daughter, Elizabeth Mary who was now fourteen and quite capable of running the home on her own. This left Ann and Maud free to focus on looking after the Hurst house, and gave the twins a break from a nasty atmosphere which was taking some time to disperse.

Maud plunged her hands down into the basin, working the lye soap into her shifts. There was a sheen of sweat across her forehead. She was used to this work, familiar with the process. When she had been younger she seemed to do nothing but the endless laundry process, her hands cracked and her knuckles swelling from the hot water, the chemicals, the scrubbing and the general submersion in water all day. It wasn't good for the skin, but it was hard physical work that distracted the mind from wandering.

Still, she couldn't help but go over the last week. It had been terrifying and intense, and she was left confused and unsettled, not so much by what Hobart had done, but by what had happened after he had gone.

He had simply informed her that Ellen's future was in her hands, and walked away. Maud remained in the barn in the hay, not sure if she had the strength to get up. How would she look Ellen in the eye now, after what had happened? She had allowed the maid to treat her as inferior all these years, and now Ellen had seen her beaten by her husband and thrown out of the house for the night. As if she was a flea-bitten disobedient dog. If it had been uncomfortable with Ellen before, she dreaded to think what life would be like now.

The barn door creaked open quickly as Amos Cornforth opened the door, unaware Maud was there. He marched in before seeing her and stumbling to a halt. Maud lowered her hair, thankful that her messy loose hair would shade her face. There was a great weight of shame pressing down on her. That she was an unworthy woman, beaten by her husband. Unable to control staff or run a household. A mess of a woman.

Amos forgot himself, his rank and status, and hurried to Maud, dropping to his knees before her. "Mrs Hurst, are you quite well? What's happened?"

Oh no, not pity, Maud thought as she felt her eyes well up with tears. She couldn't cope with this. She moved to try and tell him to go, but instead he saw the flaring purples of bruises on her face.

"Have you been attacked?" He took hold of her face gently, forgetting for now his position as employee of this woman's husband. He brushed the hair back from her face to inspect the damage. She would not meet his eye. "I've always worried about you, what with your husband being away so much. Was it thieves?"

She had to squash this now or there'd be all kinds of tales of highwaymen and bandits circulating the village, and probably the neighbouring settlements along the valley, before the day was out. "A man has a right to discipline his wife," she said quietly, hoping that would be enough. He would remember she was married, realise she was a disgrace and get back to his work.

Amos took a sharp breath and lowered his eyes. He was still holding her by the shoulders. She felt so frail, the sense of bird-like bones beneath the fabric and skin under his hands. "If you were my wife, I'd never hit you."

Maud started to shake. She couldn't take this. He ought not to show her kindness. "How can you stand this?" she wailed at him. He looked at her in bewilderment. "How can you stand to be here, living in this village, working for... for him?"

"This is all I know."

"But this was your family's home, and look what you are reduced to. Why did you never just move away?"

He smiled sadly. A lot of the locals had wondered about this. And not just over his misfortune and the fact that he stayed, but the simple fact that he took it all with such good grace, with not a drop of bitterness in his heart. "And where would I go? And what would I do?"

Maud had no answer to that. She knew the world was cruel to those at the bottom of the hierarchy. Those without family, those without money. Penniless and without a benefactor, many lives were hopeless through no fault of their own. Yet folks with better situations would look down upon them as though they had brought it all upon themselves, as if there were one of the animals, not quite a human. Certainly not in the way they were. She'd never had anything much before Hurst had come along, and when he'd said he would marry her, she was in such a dire circumstance that it really had been her only option. She tried to be good and meek, grateful for the luck he had brought her. Yet when she remembered what had happened before, she would still feel anger.

"How can you stand it?" she asked. "You out of your family home, and us living here? How can you be happy?"

"I am happy to know you have a home here. I am only sorry it is not as safe a home as you deserve."

She lowered her eyes. She would have to get out of this barn and back to the house. If they stayed here, talking like this, who knew where things would end. She couldn't keep her defence against Amos' kindness and warm hands indefinitely. "I need to go in."

"Of course." He helped her to her feet, catching her arm when she seemed to buckle. A woman in her condition should never have been left out here over night. He didn't know what she supposedly had done to deserve such wrath, but he couldn't imagine anyone like Maud doing anything particularly wicked on purpose.

Together they slowly walked across to the house, his arm about her waist to steady her. What on earth would Ellen have to say about this arrangement if she came out now and saw her? There'd be more beatings, but not just about the maid stealing the lady of the house's property. Disobedient staff was one thing, but gossip of infidelity was as good as a hanging offence.

Of course Ellen never did see them together, outside in the yard. When they entered the house they found her shivering and clammy, laid out on the kitchen table like a sickly ham hock dressed in clothes. She whimpered and sobbed when she heard footsteps approaching. Maud gasped when she saw the girl's bloodied legs hanging over the table. The flesh was red and swollen, and on the left it looked as though a shard of bone was sticking out of the skin. In comparison Maud had escaped with the lightest of beatings.

There was a cough in the doorway, and they turned to see Old Marsden, lit up by the morning light. Her shawl was over her head to keep the morning chill out of her ears. A covered basket was hooked in the crook of her arm. She was wiser than any of them, already aware of the dynamics of these people, of their pasts and their futures. "Mrs Hurst," she spoke. "I believe I could aid you with some injuries and fatigue you may be suffering."

Maud stared at her. "How did you...?"

The old woman stepped into the house. "I just had a feeling I was needed." She looked over at Amos, "Haven't you got sheep to be tended?"

He snapped out of his day dream, perhaps realising just how inappropriate some of his actions had been this morning. "Yes, of course." He went for the door, pausing before departure to look back at Maud. "If you need anything, just call."

Maud nodded.

"Now, let's take a look at those bruises."

Maud gestured towards Ellen, but Old Marsden continued as though there was nothing more than a chicken waiting to be plucked on the kitchen table. She led Maud through to the sitting room and away from the sight, so that they might tend to her bruising and take something to settle her nerves.

"I know a lot of men have struck out at their wives or maids at some point," Ann started as she wrenched heavy, sodden cloth from the rinsing barrel. "But what he did to Ellen was very savage."

Maud glanced up at her from her work.

Ann misread the stare. "I'm not saying she didn't deserve it."

"No one needs a beating like that." Maud paused in her work. "She'll probably walk again, but she'll be crippled for the rest of her life."

"She's not known her place from the moment she came to Colmondale."

"We both come from the same place."

Ann wrinkled her brow. "You two don't talk the same."

Maud smiled and looked down at her red hands. The skin was all shrivelled and wrinkled from having been in the water so long. "I don't mean that. I come from West Riding, from a village called Haworth."

"Long way from here?"

She nodded.

"What's it like?"

"Similar to this. We have our fields and our moors on the tops of the hills. It's rockier like, I mean, the earth seems different. Maybe it's because we're further from the sea..." she drifted off. She had never been home since Hurst brought her here over six years ago. "But you can't think ill of Mr Hurst," she continued, her thoughts switching from home to her husband. "He was brutal, but he has shown me great kindness in the past and I am forever in his debt. I was a maid, just like Ellen, before I married."

This didn't surprise Ann that much. Maud knew too much of the practical things in running a home to make her think she was a highborn lady. She'd always been too ready to get stuck in and do the hard graft. And any woman who had hands like those hadn't been born in a state of luxury and money.

"The twins..." Maud started, words tumbling from her mouth without a thought. These things ought not to be spoken of, for society was unforgiving and strict, especially when it came to a woman's sins. Yet she had no one to really talk to, and had kept so much to herself, almost burying her true self somewhere, and just robotically working through the days and months. "You see, I got myself with child out of wedlock. Not on purpose, you understand, but it happened and..."

"And Mr Hurst married you," Ann finished for her.

"Does this shock you?"

Ann shrugged. "The church preaches that people should wait but there are plenty I know who had a baby on the way and a rushed marriage. Round here we're all farming stock so you don't see much social climbing that way. But he did the honourable thing and married you when he got you in that position. I can imagine there'd be plenty of merchants and traders who would have just left you to it. They travel so much, it'd be easy done."

Maud opened her mouth to correct Ann of one false assumption, that Hobart was the father of the twins, but stopped herself. That might be a revelation too far, even for Ann who seemed understanding of life.

Ann broke out in a grin. "Besides, a lot of it is luck isn't it, for those of us who had our children in wedlock. It could have just as easy happened before."

Maud smiled. "Yes, I suppose you're right."

The Hurst's family home, the farmstead that had once belonged to the Cornforths, stood out on moorland at the edge where the grassy fields met the peaty rough landscape, covered by the low-lying shrubby heather that rolled out for miles, flowering purple in late summer. There was a track close by that headed into the village of Colmondale, as it was originally called, although gradually the name Commondale was taking over as travellers, drovers and newcomers misheard and mispronounced. The main body of the village was a scattering of cottages deeper into the steep sided valley, many close to the little river that would flood at times in winter and spring with the melting of the snows. Ancient trees were scattered with the houses and along hedgerows. There were kitchen gardens and small fields of produce for the locals. There was an inn, The Cleveland Inn, and a bleaching mill further downstream where the locals could take their homespun cloth for bleaching. There was no church, for the village was too small to support a priest. For religious blessing and spiritual salvation, the locals either had to walk four miles up over the moors to the north to Moorsholm to attend St Marys, or follow the river valley for another four miles to the village of Danby who had St Hildas. There had been an old hermitage in the valley which was connected to the priory over at Guisborough, but this had long since fallen into disuse with the dissolution of the monasteries a couple of hundred years ago. Colmondale lay on the route between Guisborough and Whitby, both of which had been important ancient religious sites.

Of all of Ann Longbottom's children, it was William, now sixteen and apprenticed to the blacksmith, who was the most religious. Never a week went by when he did not walk the distance to attend church services, regardless of the weather or his own health. Gilly Longbottom, seven, and her little friend Gillian Hurst, six longed to follow him every Sunday but were too small to keep up. Instead they had to make do with idolising him from afar, and walking with Ann Longbottom. Ellen Withers and Maud Hurst attended church sparingly, especially in winter when the snows could virtually make the family housebound. Illness came so frequently that they did not always dare to step outside when it did not feel necessary. They were not always easy times, and only last year the Longbottoms had lost their son, David, only four to influenza.

That summer's day, whilst Ann was up at Long Pines helping Maud Hurst, Elizabeth Mary, now fourteen and feeling in her prime, reigned over her other siblings. After William she was the eldest, and as the eldest girl, it was her right to rule the kitchen in her mother's absence. Just outside from the kitchen, in sight from the open back door, she could see her younger sister Gilly, along with Gillian Hurst, podding peas and quietly getting on with their chores. Neither girl was any trouble, and although she would cast an eye in their direction now and then just to be sure, she always knew where they'd be. Well behaved, quiet and predictable.

It was quite odd to think how siblings born of the same parents and brought up in the same environment could be so different. Her other sister, Mary, now eleven, was a bolschy little child, never quiet and always running about, sticking her nose into other people's business and generally getting under folk's feet. It was Mary who had started the trend of referring to Mr Hurst as The Hob. Although no one would ever dare say such a thing to his face, even a few of the adults in the village had picked up the habit. It was so stupid; everyone knew hobgoblins were just stories to scare children. Elizabeth Mary had almost convinced herself of the fact, although on dark and windy nights, the strange noises outside would sometimes scare her. And she knew that some of the older women still left out bits of food for the goblins, in thanks for the chores they did, and to keep them sweet.

Despite the age difference, for six and eleven were like centuries apart as far as children were concerned, Mary Longbottom had rather taken to Eleanor Hurst, and the two would often be seen in one another's company. Eleanor Hurst was a hopeless child with her head in the clouds. It was a wonder she hadn't been lost on the moors yet, and Elizabeth Mary was quite sure that sooner or later she would break her mother's heart.

Mary and Eleanor were out in a small grassy meadow where the pony was kept, picking daisies to make into chains. Mary had said that they would be able to give the chains to the hobgoblins, and they would grant them wishes. Eleanor had never heard of hobgoblins granting wishes, but Mary was eleven and must know what she was talking about.

Pulling up a handful of daisies, Eleanor ran up the slope to her friend. Her bonnet had long since bounced off the back of her head, and was only clinging on by the ribbons tied under her chin. The bonnet flew out behind her like an oddly shaped cape. Her childish breathing forewarned Mary that she was coming.

"Look." She thrust the fistful of daises forward. "These are really big. Do you think we'll get special wishes?"

Mary inspected the flowers. "Maybe." She didn't sound convinced. She broke out into a grin and looked slyly over at Eleanor. "Of course, you might be able to arrange things with the hobs."

"Me?" Eleanor's eyebrows shot up. "Because I live closer? Amos showed me where their hills are."

"No, silly," Mary giggled. "Everyone knows your pa is a hob."

"He is not." Eleanor did not like talking about her father. Theirs was an odd, formal relationship, and he had little to do with his daughters when he was at home. He was the same as some of the other fathers she saw in the village, only that they were at home every day. And there were others who would talk to their children, pick them up, play in their games. They were like Amos.

"Is too," Mary retorted. "He's not normal sized, is he?"

"Hobs don't live in houses."

"Yours isn't in the house that much. He's always scuttling off onto the moors."

"He's going to the coast on business. He's a merchant."

"He's a hob. I bet if you go out at night you'll see him sitting on his hill playing his fiddle."

Eleanor dropped down into the thick grass, a perturbed look on her face. What if Mary was right and her father was a hobgoblin? He was a bit smaller than most men, and he did have a big head. She was never sure where he went, only that he was gone a lot and the household tended to sigh in relief when he departed. Especially after that horrible night when he'd beaten mamma and Ellen. Ellen wasn't able to walk yet and just stared miserably out the window whilst she carded wool. She wouldn't make any dolls or play either anymore.

"If my father's a hob," Eleanor started. "Does that mean I'm a hob?"

Mary seemed a little stumped by this question. She dropped down into the grass by her little friend and pondered the question. In truth the impression she'd always taken of hobgoblins from the stories were that they were much smaller than normal folk, maybe the size of cats or something like that. She didn't suppose people and tiny people could have children, but she could hardly admit to that now. She'd told everyone she knew that she thought Hobart

Hurst was a hobgoblin and to backtrack would make her look foolish.

"No," Mary decided. "Because your mother's not a goblin, is she?"

"No, I suppose not." Eleanor looked down at the daisies in her lap. "So does that mean I'm a cross breed? A hublin?"

Mary laughed. "No, it just means you're daft in the head."

What Hobart Hurst had lacked in fatherly love and attention in regards to the twins, he swiftly made up for when the next child, his child was born.

Clara was the girl's name, and she was trouble from the moment of conception. She wore her mother out during pregnancy and caused a particularly troublesome birth, a fact which surprised most women in the dale. Surely a woman who had already birthed twins wouldn't have any trouble in that way now, especially when she only carried one babe.

Clara did not like to be ignored. She was a beautiful and radiant baby whilst faces doted on her, but the moment of distraction set her off biting and screaming. Her greed knew no end. Her father was more than happy to take his share of caring for the baby, another fact that had the women of the dale shaking their heads and raising their eyebrows. Babes were not men's premise. It certainly was a very odd carry on.

When the infant was eight months old, Hurst decided that his wife had been stuck in Commondale for too long, and took her away to stay with a business contact who had made the offer of a visit during the summer. Hobart, Maud and Clara were gone from the dale for two months, socialising with finer folk, where the women had little more to do than drink tea and gossip, and the men count their riches pouring in from the estates. Somehow Hurst had ingratiated himself in many fine local circles.

The twins and Ellen, who was now hobbling about, remained in Commondale. Gillian was not upset by being left behind, for she would not be parted from Gilly and William Longbottom, but Eleanor felt aggrieved. The twins were seven. Why should a baby get to travel when they should not? Why did father favour that screaming brat more than her and her sister? She refused to do her chores and spent even more time wandering the moors. Ellen had enough to worry about, what with her work taking much longer on account of her mobility issues. She had Gillian to help out, and if Eleanor wanted to run about like a little heathen, then let her.

Eleanor took her rag dolls out onto the moorland for company. She told the dolls all the stories about hobgoblins she had heard. She showed them her favourite places and secret hiding holes. They went down to the stream on hot days and dibbled their toes in the cold water. One day, on approaching the farmhouse, she realised that she had dropped one of her dolls. She looked from Annabel to Marian and scolded them for not telling her that Sarah had wandered off. She went back along the route she had taken from the stream, where she remembered Sarah with her feet in the water, but the doll was nowhere to be seen. Eleanor stood on the banks of the stream and started to sob, guessing that Sarah must have wandered too far out into the water and had been swept away.

She ran back to the farmhouse in tears, babbling a confused story about a lost doll to Ellen who wasn't really listening, and begged her to make another one. Ellen was tired and grumpy and told her she was getting too old for dolls. She ought to be more like her sister, Gillian, who had been a good little girl and stayed and helped poor old Ellen all day long. Gillian, perched on a little milking stool by the range, was licking a piece of bread dipped in honey, and grinned smugly at her sister. Eleanor started to wail at a pitch that would have shattered glass, and was sent to her bed without supper.

Later that night, when the buildings were locked up and the household was fast asleep, Eleanor was woken by a tapping sound. She sat up, looking around the darkened room and not really seeing anything. Gillian was asleep by her side.

The tapping persisted. It sounded like pebbles against glass. Many children would have been terrified of robbers and goblins at this time of night and hidden under the bedclothes. Eleanor did not give it a thought, instead getting out of bed and padding across the cold floor to the window. She pressed her nose to the glass and peered outside. The moors were lit up by a full moon. Just outside on the windowsill sat Sarah the doll.

When Hobart and Maud Hurst returned with their baby daughter from their coastal stay with well-to-do friends, the dynamics in the household shifted. Hurst was at home more frequently, and on arrival had brought out a very fine pair of children's shoes for Clara's dainty feet. The child was starting to walk, if a little inelegantly, and it wouldn't do for her to run around in her stocking feet. The child laughed and beamed, the summer light pouring through the window and lighting up her angelic curls. All the adults in the house couldn't take their eyes from the golden child.

For a short time Eleanor sulked in the kitchen, shaking her head at her tatty dolls, and looking from her own scruffy shoes to

Gillian's equally simple footwear. She did not understand why Clara was treated with such obvious preference, for she was certainly no better than the twins. And it wasn't their fault they had been born with such dark hair.

Gillian did not appear to be as worried, and in fact doubled her efforts in her chores and helping to win praise that way. She did not mind that Clara received better shoes and dresses, even though she was still just a stupid baby and couldn't really appreciate her gifts. Gillian would say that William said... and Eleanor would stop listening. Even at the tender age of eight, Gillian was becoming such a sanctimonious old woman. She loved going to church and thinking about the bible because that was what William did. Eleanor hoped it would soon stop, because William was a young man of eighteen and would soon get himself a sweetheart. Then he'd stop taking his sister Gilly, and Gillian to church, or spend so much time on instructing them on how to be good little Christians.

When Hobart Hurst scolded Eleanor for day dreaming and not completing her chores, she found that she couldn't stand to be at the farm at all. She was compared to her sister, and not in a favourable light. He then told them that they needed to learn the running of a house so that they would make good wives. Gillian had looked dreamy, probably thinking of William. Eleanor stuck her bottom lip out and said it didn't matter, because there wasn't anyone to marry in Commondale. Hurst told her that he intended to marry them to sons of important trading contacts, at which point she had screamed and stamped her feet and told him she was never marrying some shopkeeper's son. She was thoroughly thrashed and told to go clean out the chickens, but instead she gathered up her dolls and fled to the hills.

It was August and the sun was blazing across the moorland. The earth was dry and copper brown, the scrubland heather in full bloom painting the rolling tops of the hills a vibrant purple. As Eleanor walked through the sprawling open landscape, following sheep trails, her skirts brushed past the heather, setting loose clouds of sweet heather scent. The honey would be good this year. Pipits darted out of a hummock of heather to her left, bobbing and tweeting as they flew across the skyline before disappearing into the bushes. Somewhere two grouse exchanged guttural chatter. The sky was a brilliant blue with light clouds, like pulled out pieces of sheep's wool, drifting across the heavens.

Eleanor's face was firmly set, her mouth tightly pressed together to stop her lips quivering and the tears pouring. Her rump still smarted from the thrashing she'd received from disrespecting her father. She would probably be in trouble again when they found out she hadn't cleaned out the chicken hutch, but she didn't care. Clutching her ragdolls, she marched out into the isolated moorland, territory of sheep and ground nesting birds.

Sweat built on her brow as her dark hair soaked up the sun's rays. Feeling thirsty, she changed direction towards a hidden little dell she knew of. The dip in the ground was barely noticeable at a distance due to the unending spread of purple heather. But the ground did roll downwards into a tiny steep valley were a spring bubbled up. At the bottom, after a short, sharp scramble, the ground changed from heather to green grass, and old gnarled mountain ash trees, thick with lichen. Some roots came out of the ground at the edges of the little beck. Lining her dolls up by a fern growing in the dank shade, Eleanor knelt down beside the stream and lent forward, scooping fresh spring water up into her mouth.

When she sat up she gasped to see someone sitting on the opposite side of the stream. It was another little girl, around the same age, but not a child Eleanor had ever seen in the village before. She had large round eyes, a broad mouth and red swollen knuckles that looked like the hands of a little girl who always did her chores no matter the weather or damp. Her most striking feature was her long loose hair, completely uncovered, and a blonde grey colour that had a silver sheen when the sun hit it at the right angle.

For a few minutes the two little girls stayed very still and regarded one another. The girl with the silver hair broke out into a wide grin. Eleanor smiled back. "I'm Eleanor Hurst, pleased to meet you," she said, remembering her manners on how one ought to greet a stranger for the first time.

The other girl just giggled at the formality.

"Are you new here? I've never seen you in the dale."

"No," the girl spoke. "I've been here longer than you have."

"Oh." Eleanor squinted at her, wondering if she had seen her before. Definitely not, although there was something oddly familiar about her. "Who are you?"

"I'm Atheleys."

"Atheleys," Eleanor repeated. "I've never met anyone called Atheleys before."

Atheleys giggled.

"Do you want to meet my dolls?" She scrambled around to collect her treasures from under the fern. "This is Annabel. This is Marian," she explained as she laid them out in front of her knees. "And this is Sarah."

"I know, I've seen her before."

Sarah regarded Atheleys but her face remained blank and she did not acknowledge her.

"What are you doing?"

Atheleys shrugged. "Just wandering. What are you doing?"

Eleanor looked down at her dolls. "I left home. They're mean to me."

"You'll have to go back for the night. You can't stay out here forever. There are monsters."

Eleanor snorted, thinking back on all of Mary Longbottom's stories of hobgoblins. "There are not."

"There are too. There are plants that eat creatures."

"Liar."

"Am not." Atheleys sat back on her haunches. "Follow me. I'll show you."

Eleanor gathered up her dolls. "I'm not sure," she faltered. She didn't think there were meat eating plants, but what if there were? She'd heard the adults talking now and then of men who had died on the moors, especially at winter. They'd tried to cross the moors to go somewhere. But they never reached their destination. What had happened? Maybe there were things out there that would eat a man.

Atheleys giggled again. "You're not scared, are you?"

"No."

"Then follow me."

Atheleys ran up the steep slope as if made of the very air. Eleanor hung back for a moment, before pushing her dolls into her pinafore pocket and jumping over the stream. Atheleys was waiting for her at the top. A light breeze rippled through her hair, making it look like a long flag. Eleanor pushed her way through the thick heather to join her.

Atheleys grinned. "This way."

The two girls ran back out onto the tops of the hills, whooping with joy as they jumped over large hummocks of heather. They disturbed low-lying grouse who would leap up at the last minute in a flurry of brown feathers and scolding clucking, to fly low to another safe hiding place. Sheep glanced up in disinterest, occasionally moving out of the way if they thought the girls might come too close. They followed sheep trails cutting through the heather before coming out onto a paved pathway running across the moors, giving safer passage to walkers through the boggy sections during inclement weather. They ran along the hot stones, worn smooth by many footsteps, before Atheleys led the way off a side track into a boggy area, currently dry from the hot summer.

"Look."

The two girls crouched around a small clearing in the heather, where short, rabbit-nibbled grass and cushions of thick moss grew, and a collection of tiny plants barely holding themselves up from the lay of the land. Atheleys pointed at the little, vivid green plants. They had round green disks on the end of stems. The disks were covered in fat red hairs, with what looked like glistening red droplets on the tips.

"They're sticky."

Little fingers gently reached down and brushed against the little sundew plants.

"Bugs and flies get stuck here and the plants eat them."

"Eww."

"Everything has to eat something."

In the late afternoon they sat upon a heathery mound in a line, Eleanor's dolls laid out to take in the sun. There was a small cairn of stones close by where an adder had been basking into the sun until the girls had arrived and disturbed the lazy slumber. Eleanor abruptly ducked down into the heather.

"What is it?" Atheleys looked from her new friend to the expanse of moorland. Her sharp eyes picked up movement and saw a figure walking up the bank. He was not heading in their direction, but would pass by at a couple of hundred metres. He was not a particularly tall man, but had a disproportionately large head. He walked with a stick and carried a well packed satchel. He walked a lot on the moors.

"I don't want him to see me," Eleanor whispered.

"He won't see you," Atheleys said. She watched the figure observing his surroundings, and he did indeed look towards the mound, but nothing he saw made him change his course. She giggled. "He has a funny head."

Eleanor sat up. "He's my father."

"He's a hob."

Her eyebrows shot up. "Did Mary Longbottom tell you that?"

"He looks like an overgrown goblin."

The evenings were long and light, but there came a point at which Eleanor realised she should probably go back to the farm. She'd seen the Hob, as she liked to refer to him as when she was annoyed with him, leave. He probably wouldn't be back for days. And perhaps now her mother would notice she was missing, if she wasn't too busy with Clara.

"I should go home now," Eleanor said as she stood up. "Are you going home?"

"Will you come back up here?"

"I'm always up here."

"But you'll come back and play with me?"

Eleanor smiled. "Yes. You'd better go home too, or else your mamma will be worried about you." She ran down the mound and across to the path, before turning back at waving at Atheleys. Atheleys sat and watched her until she went around the curve of the hill and disappeared from view. She did not leave the mound.

Mr Meriwether came to the Hurst family shortly after Clara had turned five. He was a contact of Mr Hurst's down in London, and had been persuaded to come north for several months. Who knew what fee Hurst had been required to pay to entice the gentleman to Yorkshire, or what secrets he had threatened to divulge. But come Mr Meriwether did, and he was pleasantly surprised by the clear air, hot sun and beautiful wilderness of the moors. He took to hearty walks before breakfast, and paid one of the Longbottoms, eight year old Abraham, to show him some of the local pathways until he got to know the few miles around the Hurst house well enough to go out on his own. In inclement weather, a stranger could get lost on the moors, although Atheleys and Eleanor, watching from the heather mound, usually had a good idea of where he was during his ambulations.

Mr Meriwether, an older gent with static-filled waves of grey hair like the sea waiting to crash into the shore of his forehead, was a new spectacle for the farming folk of Commondale. In his late fifties, and in fact only a couple of years senior to his employer, he cut the figure of a gentle and well bred fellow, in well tailored suits, fine polished shoes and handkerchiefs the women of the dale could not even dream of owning. He was given a room in the Pines Lodge farmstead, and on an evening, with a drop of port to warm his imagination, he could talk until dawn about the people he had known and the places he had been, regardless of whether all of his tales were strictly speaking true. When her work was done, Ellen would sit wide eyed as she listened. Evenings were spent in the kitchen. Hurst was away a lot, and Mrs Hurst naturally gravitated to the kitchen regardless that the study would have been more fitting for a lady of her position. Not wanting to be seen a snob, and always keen for an audience, Mr Meriwether joined them in the kitchen, thinking that such a thing would never have happened in London. He would have barely seen the likes of Ellen Withers, with her grotesque limp and thudding footstep in a decent London household.

Now that Clara was walking and talking, Hobart Hurst had seen the need to develop her good breeding. Whilst Maud could lead by example with good manners and etiquette, much of which she had developed during their years of marriage, in the arts she was severely lacking. Mr Hurst was conscious that young ladies needed accomplishments. Mr Meriwether, a tutor in music and art, was to deal with just that issue.

Initially he was only employed to teach Clara, but with some persuasion on Maud's part and the point in fact that they would not get their money's worth if Clara was the only pupil, Hobart Hurst agreed that Eleanor and Gillian could also benefit of their summer visitor.

Clara was the most delightful of all three pupils, and yet the least diligent. Maud had told her husband that their daughter was still too young to apply herself properly to lessons, but he was determined that his daughter would be the finest lady in the county. Clara certainly looked angelic as she sat in the study with the mandolin delicately set in her lap and the sunlight backlighting her blonde curly hair. She smiled like a cherub and would strum her finger through all the strings. It was neither a note nor a tune, but the image would have Mr Meriwether clapping in delight. Clara would then jump up and run through the house to whoever she came to first, Maud or Ellen, and demand that did they not agree, she looked like sweetness itself with her new little mandolin. Maud would kiss her on the top of her head, and Ellen would smile and say she must be from heaven itself. Somewhere in the shadows Eleanor stuck her tongue out unnoticed.

Gillian refused point blank to have anything to do with the music lessons on offer, and would piously help with kitchen chores as if she had been born a scullery maid and not a gentleman's daughter. Maud tried in vain to explain to the eleven year old that she did not need to do these things, but Gillian was stubborn and found peace in the humility of good simple work. She could not be a fine lady, because fine ladies did not consort with blacksmiths.

But some afternoons she was gradually tempted to do a little drawing, and Mr Meriwether was particularly impressed by her eye for detail and ability to capture what she saw on paper. Gillian was equally impressed by her undiscovered talent, and in secret moments put it to good use drawing William's likeness, which she kept locked away in her little chest.

Eleanor needed little encouragement, and Maud was quietly pleased to see how the wild roaming of the moors reduced as she spent time dedicated to her lessons. Out of the three children, it was Eleanor who took most from the education offered. In drawing she was enthusiastic but childlike and would only make an average accomplishment of the art. But whilst Clara posed with her mandolin, Eleanor picked up the violin and there was rarely a day when she did not have the instrument jauntily set under her chin. After a few weeks of the cat-screaming-torture, she gauged the finger placement and bow movement correctly, and suddenly sweet music poured forth. She learned to read music, and when Mr Meriwether realised how poor her actually reading and writing was, he made sure she caught up in that regard as well. Eleanor had a particular ear for music, and could pick up a tune hummed or tapped, and adapt it quickly to the violin. Mr Meriwether had morose moments, wondering what Eleanor Hurst could have become if only she lived among civilised folk, but her father was determined to keep the family out in the moorland. He would let Gillian and Eleanor learn enough to make them good wives for contacts' sons, but it was only Clara he sought to really cultivate.

On the long summer evenings with the night only really coming past ten, Eleanor would wander up into the moors and sit with Atheleys. The two girls would sit and kick their heels against the peaty, bracken earth, or dance around the mound whilst Eleanor played the fiddle. Atheleys didn't play anything, or so she said, and was unable to join in for a duet, but she taught Eleanor reels and jigs, slow sad songs and upbeat melodies, Eleanor committing them to memory and the violin's strings. Amos Cornforth would joke with her some mornings after that he had thought her a hobgoblin, hearing music drift across the moors and seeing a figure on a hillock, before he realised it was Miss Hurst. And of course she was too fine a little girl to be a goblin.

Eleanor had looked him in the eye and said: "Who says goblins are horrid in appearance?"

He smiled, a little bemused by the child, and looked up to find Maud Hurst in the doorway. Nerves overcame him and he didn't know where to look, just as Maud found herself looking to the doorway and the hinge of the door. Then Mr Meriwether arrived whistling from his morning exercise and it was time to go in and take breakfast. Inside Clara held up her mandolin to Ellen Withers and sought reassurance that it was a far sweeter sound than the violin.

Autumn came and Mr Meriwether packed up his belongings, satisfied with what he had read in the papers and that 'it' had all blown over. It was time to return to civilisation and London. He had suggested to Hobart Hurst that Eleanor might benefit from a visit to the great city, and he knew of an excellent musical school for girls where her talent could bloom. No such offer was made for Clara, which soured Hurst's countenance. Clara was still too young to be parted from her mother, Mr Meriwether quickly added, tripping up on his mistake. Hurst was not to be persuaded, and Mr Meriwether travelled back south on his own. The mandolin and a begrudged violin were purchased from the music tutor, along with sheet music to help the girls continue to develop their musical skills, or lack thereof.

The day after the personable tutor had left their closed little world forever, Gillian and Eleanor were walking back up to the farmhouse from the village. One would assume that twins were close and constantly together. In truth the two girls were often apart and seemingly quite disinterested in the other's mindset. Yet they were quite confident in their separation, and there wasn't a thing that anyone could say about the other twin that would have surprised them. Identical at birth, yet they looked like two very different aspects of one personality. Gillian had very neat clothes, her hair carefully brushed and pinned back under her bonnet. She was patient and hardworking, always putting any pleasure to one side in favour of duty. As well as her folder of drawing papers she carried a basket full of apples Ann Longbottom had offered the family. In contrast Eleanor was scatterbrained and mentally wandering the moors in solitude even now, wisps of hair pulled loose from her plait and blowing in the breeze. Her clothes and her general demeanour had a kind of rustled look, as if she was itching to break free. A bag of apples swung by her side, and it was purely by good luck that the bottom of the bag never hit the rocks in the path.

Up ahead William and his younger sister were walking at a merry pace towards the village. William carried a bag of tools, Mary a bag with the remains of their food. Just behind them they were accompanied by another figure, a young woman with autumnal glistening brown hair and cheery red checks. They had never seen her before, but as they slowed Eleanor could sense her sister growing tense. Suddenly they felt every one of their short eleven years.

"Eleanor!" Mary shouted as she recognised the girl. She had not seen her friend from up the hill quite so much in the past year. She knew that the Hurst girls had a tutor over the summer, and had been occupied in their lessons. One might have assumed that between learning to be a lady and learning to run a household, there wasn't much time for gallivanting with childhood friends. In fairness Mary's own childish free time had diminished extremely.

She was sixteen and worked as a maid at the public house close to where they lived. There was no time for games and childish laughter anymore. People looked at her as a woman now. Marriage was murmured about, although she had no interest in being tied down. Now that she was old enough to have a job, to get out of the house and even the village without her mother, she felt as though she was only truly starting to live. This was why she had agreed to help her brother today.

Eleanor waved to Mary. "Where are you folks coming from?"

"Chequers," Mary said as the two parties met, coming to a halt.

"Chequers?"

"That's the drover's inn, isn't it?"

"Aye," William acknowledged the question, smiling in Gillian's direction and saying a quiet hello. "Up on the hills above Osmotherley. The blacksmith over there is not well and they had the cattle drovers in. There were a few that needed re shoeing."

"I thought only people and horses got shoes," Eleanor snorted.

"No, silly," Mary retorted, moving over to the as yet unnamed woman, and taking something out of the bag the stranger carried. Gillian watched the familiarity between the stranger and Mary, and the obvious fact that whatever was in that bag was to do with William's work. She felt her eyes narrow.

"Osmotherley's a long way from here," Gillian said.

William nodded. His smile radiated happiness. "It's a good six hour walk from here."

"Especially with all these tools!" Mary laughed. "Lucky thing Megan Hammond could come back with us to help carry them." She held out a couple of flat iron pieces, almost in the shapes of half broken hearts. "These are the shoes that go on the cattle. They've got so far to walk to get to market. They've got to wear something to protect their feet."

"Six hours is a long time," Gillian agreed, something in her voice accusing. "I would have thought there would have been other smithies closer by."

"Aye, well," William twisted to look around at the young woman Megan, and smiled. She beamed back at him. "We have a family connection back to the Hammonds, and it was a good reason to go visit at the same time."

"Do the cattle have to walk a long way?" Eleanor asked Mary.

"And now Megan has come to Commondale," Gillian pointed out.

"All the way to London town," Mary said.

"That's where Mr Meriwether has gone. And where do they come from?"

"The north."

"Do you mean the far north, like Durham where our Ellen Withers is from?"

Mary's eyes sparkled. "I mean the far, far north. They come from Scotland."

Eleanor gasped in delight. "But that's so far away. How do they manage it?"

"I should introduce you all, I'm forgetting my manners," William said. Megan giggled behind him. "Ladies, this is Megan Hammond of Osmotherley. Miss Hammond, these two ladies are Eleanor and Gillian Hurst of Pines Lodge."

Gillian made a cool but polite curtsey, nudging her sister in the side to remind her of her manners. Eleanor's thoughts were still lost to Scotland.

"It's very nice to meet you both."

"Eleanor, you shall have to come with me over to the drover's road," Mary told her. "You'll hear the most amazing stories."

"Amazing as they are, we've been walking a long time and ought to get back to mother," William said. He doffed his cap to the Hurst twins. "Ladies," he said, not meaning to be anything but a gentleman, but the word grated on Gillian. She was just still a child.

The twins stepped to the side of the road and watched the trio continue their final walk down the hill and into Commondale proper. Mary twisted around to wave back at them, shouting again that she would take Eleanor sometime. Megan fell into step with William, and told him what sweet little girls the Hurst twins were. Certainly a source of pride to any mother.

Eleanor did not look at Gillian, and Gillian did not remove her eyes from the back of Megan's head. "You don't know she's anything more than a distant relative helping with a sack of old cattle shoes. It doesn't mean anything."

Gillian pressed her lips together. "We'll see."

Maud stepped out of the kitchen, escaping the heat and the humidity and the incessant chatter of Ellen Withers. Slipping out of the front door, she stood in the front yard and felt the wind rush up from Commondale village to cool her brow. She wiped her hands on her apron. She still did too much, a lady was not supposed to work like a maid. She could not help herself. Clara would fit the role better, she was sure. The girl did precious little in the way of chores, but she was a delight to have in the house. A sweet angel. All three of her girls were lucky to be able to grow up with this kind of money backing them. Not to have to get up at five in the morning to start with cleaning out the fireplaces. To have to spend days over the household laundry, watching their hands go soft and red, the skin unable to hold up and eventually cracking. The knuckles swelled painfully. To feel the crack of the knees every time one got up from the scullery floor. And not even thirty. Already the girls had so many more advantages over their own mother, with music lessons and tutors, time to sit and read, or draw, or play the violin. And certainly when Clara was older her concentration would improve, and she would be just as talented as the twins. Each in their own special way.

Leisure time certainly allowed for the development of a personality, Maud reflected. When one's head was constantly in the running of household work, either that or so exhausted it lay upon the pillow unconscious, there was little time for reflection or to consider the world and wonder what exactly one's place was within it. Maud didn't work anywhere near as hard as she had done when she had been properly employed as a maid. With Ellen Withers and Ann Longbottom's occasional help, coupled with Gillian's diligent chores, there were times when she could step away from housework and be the lady of the house. Only that Maud never knew what to do with herself. She could sit nervously for hours in the study, looking at those books she could not read, wishing she had a bit of darning or fixing in her hands. Wondering if the world would even miss her should she disappear. Hobart would be gone for weeks, and when he was at home she was either the woman who ran the household, the thing that looked pretty in the background or the toy in the bed. As a person he had no interest in her, but then she supposed she was his inferior, and in all honesty, as she did not know herself, how could she expect more from someone else?

A wave of melancholy swamped her and she bit back her tears, looking to the moors. This would happen more often of late, a self pity that darkened her thoughts to the point she couldn't quite remember what had sparked off her desolate mindset. She was only twenty-nine and yet she felt finished with. Three children, and doubtful there would be any more, and a household that would probably continue running even after she was gone. She could walk out onto the moors right now, hunker down in the heather and disappear.

Wiping her eyes with the back of her hand, she stalked across to the barn. She would seek this sanctuary when the melancholy came upon her. It was out of the way and no one would hear her. She could sit in the hay and sob her heart out until she was dry and parched and ready to return to the routine of life. She caused no one any trouble. There was something comforting about the barn, the half light contained within, and the musty, natural scents of the hay, the creaking of the wood as the wind battered outside.

She slipped in through the doorway and a cry of anguish finally escaped her mouth. She felt her cheeks burn red, even in solitude embarrassed by her self pity. Even after all the good fortune life had given her, she was sobbing in the barn thinking life had passed her by. Her vision blurred with tears, and she wandered, almost drunkenly into the depths of the barn.

It was some minutes before there was an uncomfortable cough and a figure shifted. Maud felt her horror ball up in her throat at the realisation that there was a witness to her distraught behaviour. Amos stepped out into the centre of the barn where the light was best, looking distinctly guilty, and also saddened. She felt sick. What would people think of her now?

"I'm sorry mistress," he started. "I was already working in the barn when you came in. I don't mean to spy upon you, and I would have kept out of the way only that I need to get back outside. I can usually keep quiet and wait, as much as it breaks my heart to see you in distress."

Maud felt nausea begin to splurge in her stomach. This was far worse than she had first thought. "Usually?" How many years had she been coming her to deal with her 'moments' as she liked to think of them. "How many times have you seen..." what to call it? She felt increasingly foolish. "Seen this?"

"A number."

"And you said nothing?" she asked shrilly.

"Forgive me. I was afraid to say anything. I did not wish to frighten you, and I had a fear that if I started to speak I would not be able to stop myself. It pains me to see you like this. Is your husband still hurting you?"

A lady would have sent him packing for even hinting at a failure of the master of the house. A lady would not have started this conversation with an employee. A lady would never hide in the barn to shed her tears. Maud was no lady. Words and tears jumbled themselves together in her mouth and she could not look at him. "He does not. My husband has a great disinterest in me. And I can understand why, for I do not see the point of myself some days."

Amos stepped across the last distance between her and had the woman in his arms as she started to break down again. He stroked her hair and wiped away her tears, and when she looked up at him, he could no longer practice the discipline and self control of the last decade. He kissed her and felt her gasp and respond, fingers digging into his arms as if to reassure herself that it was not a fantasy.

Maud pulled away. "We can't."

"I'm sorry. It's entirely my fault." He could be fired for this. Thrown off from the estate, and the work. Shunned from the village. He would have nowhere to go. Worst of all, he would not see her again.

"He has been very good to me," Maud whispered of her absent husband. "He helped me when no one else would. But he does not love me." She did not let go of his arms. She had been in this position before, and knew from experience what trouble it could cause. The luck of a salvation would not happen twice. But there was a fire in her belly and her heart was beating so fast, that she was sure she would fall away if she let go now. "I have watched you all these years," she confessed. "And wondered, if things had been different, if I might have..."

His heart might break if he heard the same thoughts that ran through his mind spoken by Maud Hurst. He kissed her again and the two of them fell into the hay, for a short time lost in the world of what ifs and might have beens.

Winter came and the grown women of the household swiftly realised that Maud was with child again. They also knew that a woman ought not to be in such a condition when her husband had been absent for so long. Ellen Withers could not blame her, certainly not these days when her loyalty was most definitely realigned from Hobart to Maud since that night of the dreadful beatings. Hobart Hurst was a poor match for the young woman. Maud was not yet thirty and Hurst was already in his fifties. He was hardly present. Every woman wanted love in her life. But she ought to have kept it hidden in her heart as she had managed all these years. For she had too much to lose now, and there were the three girls to think of as well.

It was a hard winter. The snows came early and the moors vanished under thick drifts of snow. Blizzards blew horizontal across the open landscape, heaps of ice crystals piling up against the wall of the Hurst farm house, reaching the windows. Inside the fires were kept blazing, but the crackle of the fire couldn't completely blot out of the howl of the frozen winds and the patter of snowflakes battering against the windows.

Amos struggled with the sheep which were scattered over the moors. They were hardy beasts with thick woolly winter coats replenished, and of what little sense they had, most of them realised it was best to hunker down together in amongst the heather. He got most of the creatures back to the barns on the farmstead, but some perished out on the moors, frozen bodies only to be discovered in the early spring as the snows melted away to reveal sun-warmed bloating corpses.

Maud's old hairline crack in her upper jaw ached dreadfully with the chill and the pregnancy, and the terror of when Hobart Hurst would return to find his wife with a child logic said he could not have put there. The worst beating she had taken from him was after he had caught Ellen Withers dancing in the kitchen wearing the lady of the house's jewellery; and on that night Ellen had taken the worst of his temper. She did not know what would come of this situation. Old Woman Marsden had been past before the snows really got going, with her bag of herbal lore. They had talked politely, each skirting around the subject but fully aware of the predicament. The old woman had essentially offered to deal with it. She had a herbal concoction that would coax nature into disposing of the unborn, but Maud couldn't bring herself to do it. This had been the happiest conception of all, despite the deceit. Lust and love had certainly been involved with the twins, but she had been abandoned the moment she had realised she was in the family way. Clara had been created out of duty and a weighted sense of gratitude. Amos Cornforth was ever the faithful dog, at the farm every day, and struggling up through the heavy snow to make sure the women of the household had everything they needed. The last they had heard of Hobart, he had been in London, crossing over to Paris on business, and was not sure if he would make it home before yuletide. With the weather as it was now, no one would be making it across the moors to the isolated little village.

Clara was bored by being cooped in the house for so long, and without any new company, particularly of the adoring male variety, she inevitably took to causing trouble. Even her mamma did not have enough time to dote on her, with the new baby making her tired and wan. Ellen Withers was busy with the household chores and forever bringing firewood into the house, forever praising Amos Cornforth and how at least he knew how to do something right and proper. Their firewood supplies never dropped the entire winter.

The angelic child took to telling lies, many of which were never noticed due to the busy nature of the housework. Her two sisters she could never persuade in adoration, one too pious and keen on chores and horrified of vanity, the other too suspicious and contrary and keeping of odd company that Clara, even at her young age sensed was best not to meddle with.

The chicken coop was filled with extra hay for insulation, and diligently kept locked to protect against hungry and desperate foxes. Clara took to stealing a couple of eggs on a morning before Eleanor had chance to check the harvest. With a chipped china bowl she would mess about cracking the eggs by different means, pouring the contents into the bowl, sometimes with shell and stirring with a twig. Distracted Ellen would laugh that the sweet angel was baking a cake. Eleanor knew she was up to no good. She had never been fooled by that angel facade, but had never been interested enough to involve herself further. When Gillian asked her young sister what she was doing, and was informed that she was divining the future, she slapped the child and screamed at her that she must stop with these black arts before throwing the bowl out of the house. Clara turned red-faced and was inconsolable until Ellen Withers had beaten Gillian around the rump with a stick and sent her to bed without supper. After that incident Clara continued to play with the eggs, although she took to hiding them in her room and poking them with pins, testing to push salt and other substances inside.

Eleanor avoided housework as much as possible and busied herself with her reading and writing. She wrote long letters to Mr Meriwether, none of which could be sent, so by the spring she had a small novel worth of writings for her old tutor. When Mr Hurst eventually returned, he said he would take it with him to London, but burnt it in an inn fire on the spring journey to the capital. On the evenings she took to playing the violin, sometimes the sheet music left by their old tutor, or tunes he had taught her but had not written down, and often she retreated to the mental library Atheleys had sung over the summer.

In regards to Atheleys, Eleanor was particularly worried about her young friend during this bad winter. When the blizzards stopped and she was able to shove the door open against the piled snow, she would sometimes see the little figure of Atheleys scuttling across the middle distance. It didn't seem that Atheleys had any family, although whenever Eleanor asked, she would always change the subject. Eleanor would leave little parcels of food, and a jug of weak beer out in a corner of sheltered walls. Sometimes she would spy Atheleys from a distance, picking up on the offering, and occasionally the girl would approach the farmstead so that she could collect the food and talk to her friend for a short while. She would never go inside. Often Atheleys did not appear, but when Eleanor went outside the next day, the food was gone, the jug empty, and there were little marks, half filled in with snow, where feet had passed by.

This habit carried on in a fashion until Gillian noticed her sister trotting outside with yet another little parcel of food, and decided to follow her. She found her at the corner of walls, digging a hollow in the snow with her mittened hands.

"Eleanor, what are you doing? We can scare spare the food for you to be out burying it like a dog."

Eleanor glared at the walls. "It's for Atheleys. She won't get anything to eat otherwise."

Gillian rolled her eyes. "Will you stop this talk of Atheleys. You're too old for imagination nonsense."

"She's not nonsense."

Gillian gasped as Eleanor stood up. She had seen the food and for the first time made the connection with what she'd seen some of the silly old women in the village do at times. "It's pagan," she hissed, grabbing her sister at the elbow. "You're leaving food out for the little folk."

"Atheleys is as big as I am."

"You can't do this. We're a good Christian household."

"Yes I can!"

"I'll tell mamma."

The sisters struggled and started to fight in the snow, pulling at one another's arms and shawls. The beer jug got kicked and tipped over, spilling its contents into the snow, setting off a malted slushy patch of brown. With a shriek Gillian tipped her sister over, before grabbing the food parcel and running inside to tell Ellen that Eleanor was wasting food. Ellen soon hobbled outside, cursing Eleanor for making her come out onto the ice and snow and didn't she know that Ellen struggled to walk in such conditions. She pinched the girl's ear and dragged her back into the house, confining her to her room for the rest of the day.

Late at night, when Gillian was asleep and Eleanor lay awake with a growling hungry stomach, there was a tapping at the window. She got up and walked to the window, staggering back when Atheleys jumped up into her vision, hissing like a snake with red eyes flashing in fury. Her hair was loose and hung with ice crystals, her breath frosting against the glass. She disappeared from view and seemingly from the farm for the next two weeks, although every morning Amos would find his woodpile strewn across the yard, and on evenings heavy clumps of snow would suddenly tumble from the roof, down the chimney stack and extinguish one of the fires.

"She's angry, you know," Eleanor would growl at her sister, to which Gillian would retort it was all heathen nonsense. It wasn't until she went to bed to find a ball of snow melting under the covers, that her faith was shaken a little. Both twins got a thrashing for their mischief and drenching the bed in ice water. After that Gillian would turn a blind eye when Eleanor started sneaking out with food and beer again. After a couple of days of offerings, the snow stopped falling down the chimneys, and not only was the firewood no longer thrown all over the yard, but the pile was kept topped up without Amos having to chop another log for the rest of the winter.

One particularly brutal winter's night Ellen Withers sat close to the fire and examined her cracked hands. Regardless of the seasons, the clothes still needed washing and the household had to be run. But winter chills and cold water were not a kind combination. Her knuckles were fat and red, painful when she stretched out her fingers. The corners on her finger joints were full of swollen, cracked red skin. She rubbed goose fat into her hands in the hope of soothing her skin and aching joints, although as she held her hands out to the flickering flames she wasn't sure if it was the aroma of a gently roasted meat or a slackening on the pain that was relaxing her. Perhaps she'd have a fine set of roasted fingers by morning, the meat slipping off the bone and... She shuddered at the thought as if someone had walked over her grave. Her eye went to the doorway and she saw a feverish Clara in her nightdress staring intently back.

"Will you be eating man flesh, Miss Withers?"

"Clara Hurst!" Ellen jumped up from her seat in horror.

Gillian, who had been at the end of the kitchen table, quietly drawing Ellen's portrait unbeknown to the maid, quickly pulled over a drawing of holly leaves as Ellen hurried past her.

"What beastly things you say." Ellen lent over the girl and put a greasy hand to her forehead. "She's still hot," she muttered. Clara's eyes rolled in a delirious manner. "She must still be away with the fairies."

Gillian and Eleanor shared a look. No more had been said on the food left out for the other folk. Eleanor looked back to her knitting. The wooden needles seemed to be firmly fastened to one another with this knotted wool. She did not understand how Ellen and Gillian could rattle through their knitting, row after row, the needles clicking and moving like well oiled wheels on a cart. She was never going to make anyone a good wife. Ellen always joked about it as she came over to untangle Eleanor's failures. She sat and joked about the poor man who would be stuck with Eleanor as she got the woollen project started again.

Maud Hurst appeared behind Clara, suppressing a yawn. She wasn't that far on with the pregnancy. All her body craved was sleep and no matter how much she rested, she never found satisfaction.

"She's still hot," Ellen told her, looking gravely concerned as she thought on Ann Longbottom's baby Bethany, only a year old but taken by smallpox earlier this winter. With a son of twenty one, no one had expected her to have any more children. She supposed Ann wasn't that old, but Bethany had come as a surprise to everyone. Compared to some women, Ann had a good survival rate, with seven of her nine strong brood making it past those first few dangerous years. She looked back to the angelic little Clara. "She's terrible hot," she repeated, "And such a sweaty brow."

Maud checked her daughter's brow, then looked curiously at her fingers, rubbing fingertips together. It felt like fat. Ellen Withers hobbled back to the fire, rubbing her hands together. She returned to her seat close to the flames, and the cat leapt up into her lap.

"I'll take her back to bed." Maud looked down at her little girl. "Come my sweet, you're not well yet."

Eleanor rolled her eyes and yelped when she accidentally jabbed herself in the thigh with a knitting needle.

The wind howled outside, the snow battering desperately against the windows, wanting to be let in. The flames in the hearth danced against a shot of cold air that rushed down the chimney, before crackling back into their steady flow. Eleanor felt a chill creep up in the corners of the room and pulled her shawls back around her shoulders.

There was suddenly a great hammering at the door, just as the wind started to shriek. Ellen Withers leapt up yelping, scattering an angry cat out across the flagstones. "It is a beast!"

Gillian and Eleanor looked at one another grimly.

"No man would be out walking in such weather at night," Ellen continued gravely. "Whoever is at that door..."

The hammering started up again.

"We mustn't let them in."

"Whoever is at that door is in need of shelter and this is a Christian household." Gillian got up and went through to the door, wrenching up the bar and unlocking the door. The wind blew in from the black night, setting her back a couple of steps and shivering from the blast of frozen air. She squinted against the cold and the battering of snowflakes.

"And a girl child is sent to answer the master!"

A figure barely taller than Gillian pushed his way in and slammed the door shut. He stood for a moment as the tails of his overcoat settled, snow falling to the floor. Sweeping off his hat, he sent a flurry of snow across the threshold. Ellen Withers appeared, and he marched forward, passing her his satchel and walking stick.

"Master Hurst, what are you doing abroad at this time? Have you not seen the weather?" Ellen asked.

"I have a keen stick and a good memory and I was eager to return home," Hurst told her, standing in the kitchen doorway and surveying the scene. Eleanor stared up at him with a touch of disbelief. The snow could be waist deep. No one would be crossing the moors in weather like this. Certainly no one human.

He gave Eleanor a curious stare, as if to say to her that such thoughts ought to stop here and now. Gillian sneezed behind him, brushing the snow off her hair. "Why are you girls still up? The hour is late and the air is cold. The warmest place is in bed."

"They were keeping me company."

"Doing chores," Eleanor added, holding up her knitting.

He regarded the mess of wool. It would have been better if she hadn't bothered. That child would not be domesticated. Why could she not have been like her sister?

"Away to bed with you, both of you," he said dismissively, waving his hand in their general direction. "I've had a long, hard journey and I have no desire to set eyes on the likes of you two now."

Eleanor tossed her knitting into the basket and linked arms with her sister to leave the room. They were quite happy to go to bed, for the twins had always had a cool relationship with their father. They had grown up believing this simply was the way of things, which made his dotage on little Clara all the more unfathomable.

"And where is my wife?"

Maud stepped forward out of the shadows as if she had been waiting there all this time. "I am here."

"Ah, good," he turned upon her, the firelight glinting off his smile. "It has been a long time since we last met, and I am cold from my journey. We shall get us to bed as well, and you can warm me up."

Maud obediently followed, sadly wishing she could have arranged things in her life a little better. She thought of Amos Cornforth, alone in that hovel down in the bottom of Commondale. She wished he was here.

"Withers," Hurst shouted as an afterthought. "Get that kitchen in order."

After a week of his presence, Maud had to say something. She was tired and wan, and although not yet growing fat, she was most definitely pregnant. She did not know how he would react, fearful that his understanding of a woman's time would not match against the occasions he had been present in the household. Yet all she had to say was that she was with child, and he was strutting like a little rooster, muttering how quick it was, and how intuitive women were that they could tell so early on. This would be a boy, he told her, he was quite sure of it.

A boy, Maud thought, thinking that whatever it was, it was a lot more developed than Hurst seemed to think it was. She hoped he would not want to be here for the birth, for it would be happening a lot sooner than his reckoning.

Baby Stephen, a boy as Hobart had predicted, was born in the early summer the following year. Hobart Hurst missed the time of birth completely, working on the assumption that the child had been conceived far later than in reality it had.

The household was busy again with the screams of a newborn. Amos Cornforth was by the house every day on the feeblest of excuses about the running of the property. Clara was furious, for not only was she no longer the youngest treasure in the house, but her mother was distracted from her by both babe and farm worker. Ellen Withers was forever ushering the young child from her mother's way. The twins, now twelve, were more frequently out and about, and Clara found her range expanding as she would often go down to the village to see the other children. Her father had made threats of another tutor, but so far nothing had come to pass. It was felt that Clara was too young, and the twins had received enough attention already.

Not that the twins intended to remain ignorant. They wished to know beyond the isolated moorland bubble that was Commondale. Each took to broadening their horizons in different ways, and some were to prove more successful extents than others.

Gillian Hurst would still walk to and from church in Castleton with Gilly and William Longbottom. Sometimes they had a couple of other Longbottom children with them, who would walk at their own pace, not particularly interested in the godly discussions held by the three main leaders of the party. There were times when Megan Hammond of Osmotherley had come with them, although

Gillian was happy that the young woman had been absent from their walks this past month.

They would walk along the valley bottom on a track roughly following the Commondale Beck as it meandered through the forests and green fields hidden between two great heights of moorland. The beck joined the River Esk shortly before they arrived at the village of Castleton. Here they climbed up the hill into the main body of the village, then followed Danby Beck in a southerly direction until they reached the isolated little church of St Hildas. Once services were complete, they took the same route back. All were so accustomed to walking and hard work that the journey fazed none, especially in the summer when the land was reasonably dry and passage was easy going.

William was talking to Gilly and Gillian. He viewed them as two little sisters even though Gillian Hurst was no relation. They were formative minds he hoped to help form before their future husbands might complete the task and turn them into good wives. His latest educational tool was a pamphlet he had recently gotten hold of via the drovers that passed by further to the west. They overnighted at Chequers, a drover's inn and farmstead on the hills of Black Hambleton above Osmotherley. Drovers were the highway for information and news passing through the country, as well as conducting the essential matter of getting livestock to where it was needed for slaughter and eating. Gillian didn't like to focus too much on the matter that William spent increasing amounts of time over Osmotherley way, and instead tried to focus on what he was explaining to them from this pamphlet. It was a document only published last year, by John Wesley, a cleric, who had written his *Thoughts Upon Slavery*. It was all part of a growing movement to ban slavery, a terrible practice, William told the girls, that was still happening in the Americas. It all seemed too far away for it to be real to Gillian, but she listened diligently. William was only trying to improve them.

"It is not a just state of being for mankind to be in," William explained. Gillian and Gilly walked hand in hand, his own sister more distracted by gazing at the pretty flowers on the river bank. Gillian was wide-eyed and full of concentration.

"It dates back to the Romans and Greeks. But for a man to be beholden to a master, to have no control over his own destiny is an ungodly state. For everything he should do to be decided by the master..."

Gillian considered how the atmosphere in the home changed whenever her father came home. Her mother told her that he worked very hard and earned the money that kept them in the comfort they had grown up in. They all were to be very grateful for what he had given them. His business was something to do with buying and selling, but Gillian had never actually seen him do anything. Whenever he was at home her mother and Ellen were very careful to be sure he wanted for nothing. They fetched and carried whenever he snapped his fingers, often anticipating what he desired before he had even spoken.

"So you mean how my father is the master," she started uncertainly. "And mother is a slave to him."

William laughed. "No, sweet child, you are quite mistaken."

Gillian blushed furiously, both for the error and for being called a child.

"That is a woman's place, and it is just and right in the world. No, I am talking about the plight of the negro men..."

"Negro men," Gilly idly repeated, not listening to the content of William's second hand sermons anymore.

"They come from darkest Africa," William explained. "Their skin is as black as night. I am talking of their dignity and right to freedom."

"And what of the negro women?"

"Dear sweet Gillian, I think you are missing the point here. This is not a case of men and women. I'm sure the negro women are good wives to their men. I am talking of man's freedom."

Gillian remained silent for the remainder of the walk, realising that she still had much to learn. It would be better not to say anything more for fear of embarrassing herself, until she properly understood all that William had to teach them.

Whilst Gillian became quiet and more studious, Eleanor's adventures out of the house brought more noise and excitement into her life. She was starting to spend more time with Mary Longbottom, and as promised, the two girls had headed out across the moors to that place called Chequers. It was a line of stone farm buildings set in the moors. It stood by a drovers road heading across the hills, and to the south where the land flowed into the Vale of York and onwards to that great capital of the north, York. The girls walked tracks over the moors before dropping down onto the drover's road. They followed the ancient route past the heather-covered hill of Black Hambleton, and down over the Hill Beck Bridge, and up a slight rise to the inn and farmstead. In the summer with the sun high it was a beautiful place, with a fine view out west across to the agricultural lowlands, far further than Eleanor had ever been. In winter she imagined it could be even lonelier than at their own hillside home of Pines Lodge. Theirs was but a short walk down the hill to reach the village of Commondale. Here it was a higher hill and a longer walk before the little village of Osmotherley came into view.

It took them around six hours to get to the drovers' inn, and they arrived near noon. The girls had chattered a lot of the way, Mary divulging family secrets that were perhaps not meant to be shared just yet. It was as the twins had suspected, Megan Hammond of Osmotherley was William's sweetheart.

"They are betrothed," Mary babbled as the girls walked the sandy, well trodden route over sun-dried moorland. She did not see Eleanor's expression, who walked behind her when the path was narrow. "They will be wed. It's ever so romantic."

Eleanor rolled her eyes. Romance: what nonsense.

"But it will not be for a couple of years, for William wishes to save enough to keep a wife. I think he wants to start his own smithy."

"Years are a long time, especially with the distance," Eleanor mused.

"Oh, it means nothing, and they regularly make the walk." Mary looked back, grinning slyly. "He thinks we don't realise, but he goes out to meet her half way often enough. Of course they shouldn't really be doing it, not without a chaperone, but then William's so full of the church and goodness, I don't think they'd do anything they ought not to."

Eleanor gazed wistfully across the distance, thinking of her sister. She knew that Gillian suspected all of this already, but whilst no one admitted the truth, there was always hope for a young girl with a crush. She knew it was going to break her heart. "Gillian's never mentioned this to me," she started carefully, looking for particular information. "And she and Gilly are always off marching to church with William..."

"Oh yes, the godly pilgrimage," Mary snickered.

"But if he is so sweet on Megan, surely he would have mentioned it?"

"He said that he is going to tell people. But he gets so distracted with talking of other things. William thinks he has a natural understanding of folk and the world. He loves to explain." Mary's tone suggested she was not overly keen on having everything explained to her. "He gets caught up in his sermons at times. Forgets what he's about. I think he should have been a preacher and not a smithy, but of course Ma and Pa didn't have the money nor the status to be sending him off to colleges for the religious learning."

"So perhaps he will tell Gillian today?"

Mary paused as the path widened again, and the two girls walked arm in arm. "Truth is, he's afraid to. He reckons Gillian has a childish fancy on him."

Eleanor felt mortified on her sister's part. If Gillian knew that her emotions had been described as such by the object of her affection, she would be devastated.

"And he wants her to keep going with them to church, and learning about godly things. She listens ever so well. He says she's awful patient and compliant. When she's a grown woman, she'll make someone a great wife." Mary burst out into wild laughter. "Not like you and me, Eleanor Hurst; we're wild girls. We'll forget our babies by the streams and have the supper on late."

"Not me," Eleanor said stubbornly. "I want to travel. To explore."

"Explore!" Mary sounded incredulous. "Who ever heard of explorers from these parts?"

"My father travels all over the country, and even to France. And what about Captain Cook? He's been finding new lands far away from here."

"Cook's one in a million," Mary told her. "And he's a man. Only men have the stamina for travel like that. Oh, take heart, Eleanor," she added as her young friend looked glum. "You've been furthest of all the Hurst children now. You've been to St Hilda's with Gillian now and then, but Chequers is much further. This is the edge of the moors. Look out there to the distance. Those are the lowlands. Good farming land out there."

From this point they gazed out west, beyond the reaches of the moorland hills. The land went on forever. Eleanor wanted to go there. Mary gave her a nudge. "Come on, we're almost there."

When they reached the buildings of Chequers Inn, set out as a stone long house, the lady of the property was out the back hanging out freshly laundered sheets to dry. The wind was not particularly bad today considering what it could be like at this open height, but still the sheets slapped back into her face, making her curse.

Mary giggled as they heard the broad Yorkshire threats directed at bed clothes.

The woman stuck a peg onto the line with particular aggression before peering around the edge of her washing. She was a ruddy-faced woman with broad forearms and a rotund countenance of many skirts and decades of hard labour. Her black hair was dry and fizzy, popping out from under her mop cap wherever it found a chance to escape. "Mary Longbottom!" she exclaimed. "I wasn't expecting to see you. And you've brought a friend with you. Is this one of your young sisters?"

"No, this isn't one of my lot. This is Eleanor Hurst. Them that live up the hill from us."

"Oh yes," the woman nodded as if she was acquainted with the Hursts. Eleanor felt uncomfortable for a moment. Did people discuss them? Most probably, she realised. There was nothing women liked to do more when they were about their chores than talking about other people. Ellen Withers never stopped.

"I'm Mrs Barker," the woman introduced herself. "And you're very welcome here, Eleanor Hurst."

"Eleanor plays the fiddle. You remember I was telling you about it?"

"Oh yes," Mrs Barker smiled, a twinkle in her eye. "You might come and play for us some time. The only chance we get for music is when the drovers are through."

Eleanor gazed around the lonely farmstead. It looked even more isolated than her own home. They didn't get so many people passing through in Commondale. But they were close to the village there. Here there looked to be nothing beyond another twist of smoke coming up from a farmstead further down the hill and a long way off in the distance. She'd heard Mary talking of a nearby village Osmotherley, where the infamous Megan hailed from, but she couldn't see any sign of it from here. "You get a lot of people passing by?" she asked uncertainly.

"Oh aye," Mrs Barker nodded, hands on hips. "You wouldn't think it today, but sometimes it is packed with folk, and their beast as well. Drovers on the way down to the markets at York, or even further south. What a racket! All the men, and then there's the dogs, the beasts, sometimes sheep. Then there's travellers, pedlars, merchants..."

"Highwaymen," Mary threw in with a snort.

"Highwaymen?"

"Robbers." Mary's eyes widened. "They're awful dandy, but they'll rob you blind. When you're travelling on a lonely road, they'll come on with their horse and pistols and stop you."

"They'll rob us?"

Mrs Barker gave Mary a stern look. "You've got nowt worth robbing, child," she assured Eleanor.

Mary laughed. "How can you not have heard these things, Eleanor Hurst? You're not a mere babe in arms anymore. You've not heard of Dick Turpin? Money or your life?"

Eleanor blushed. She was very aware she was a child in comparison to these two women. Mary was only five years older than her, but at seventeen she had the figure of a woman. They were in different spheres of life, and no doubt Mary would soon be married and their time would be over.

"Dick Turpin's a highwayman?"

"Stand and deliver!" Mary roared.

Mrs Barker patted Eleanor's arm. "Don't you go worrying about old Turpin. They hanged that old rascal a good thirty years ago. Mary Longbottom just has too much of an excitable imagination about her." She turned to Mary. "What you need is marrying off, my girl. That'll calm you. Now, you girls want to come inside and take a little luncheon with me?"

Mrs Barker led them around to the front of the property to enter via the commercial entrance through which all guests came. Eleanor brought up the rear, and stopped as movement further back on the road caught her eye. It was not animation of an object, rather a being out on the road. It soon caught that it had been spotted and reacted to catch her attention further, yapping gleefully and picking up speed on the last stretch to the inn.

Mrs Barker stopped in the doorway and turned, squinting to look across the moors. "Now who is this coming to us?" she wondered.

The dog, which as it came closer proved to be a brown and white collie with wind-swept, wind-tangled fur and a healthy gleam in its eye, sprinted up to the women, yapping and wagging its tale furiously. It went straight to Mrs Barker, hopping up to place its paws on her knees in friendly greeting before dropping to all fours and running around Mary and Eleanor, sniffing at the strangers.

Mrs Barker laughed, "Why, Wee Jamie!" she exclaimed in merriment, watching as the dog trotted over to the water trough to quench his thirst. "It's been a while since we last saw you."

Eleanor crouched down as the dog returned to them, eager to stroke the merry beast. The tail started wagging furiously as he enjoyed the attention, licking the young girl's face to show his appreciation.

"He's young and full of beans, that one."

"And he's just come home to you. Has he been lost long?"

"He's not my dog," Mrs Barker said. "He's one of the drovers' dogs; one of the Scots, you know. MacCaskill's dog."

Mary's eyes brightened. "The drovers are coming?"

"Your directions are all shot if you think the drovers are coming now. That dog came from the south. When the drovers come, they're heading down from Scotland, from the north." Mrs Barker gave the dog an affectionate pet on the head. "The dogs often come back up on their own. Clever beasts, finding their way home from London. He's still got a fair way to get yet."

"Why doesn't he go home with his master?"

"Ah, they often stay down south for farming work in the autumn. Dogs want to get away home. Sometimes the men will take the post carriages back instead of walking. Depends how much money they've made." She shrugged. "Mind you, often than not the Scots'll walk back regardless of how much money they've made. They don't like to waste a penny where they don't need to." She laughed loudly. "Reminds me of my old father, tight as ouwt he was."

"Your father was a Scot?"

"No, he was a Yorkshireman." She turned her attention back to wee Jamie, who had now sat on his haunches in front of the lady of the house and started to whine. "You'll be a hungry boy after all that running, won't you? Don't you worry; your master's already paid for your supper. Let's see what we can find you. A nice bit of food and a nap by the fire won't do you any harm. Come along, girls," she ushered them into the inn. "We'll get this dog fed and look for a bit of sustenance ourselves."

The seasons swiftly hurried on towards winter. In the depths of autumn Gillian grew ever more despondent. William had admitted of his attachment with Megan. As much as Gillian wished to scream and claw skin from bone, she breathed deeply and remained calm and still. She pretended to be glad, if only so that their walks to church could continue for as long as possible. She listened carefully to William's lectures, and answered his questions diligently. At home she was silent and withdrawn. She no longer paid any attention to Clara, no matter how much she whined, begged and stamped her fine-heeled little feet on the flagstones. Maud and Ellen were much taken with the first little boy of the house, and what a cherub he was. When they weren't looking after the baby, Ellen was busy with chores and Maud had started to take a greater interest in the property, spending much time with their shepherd and land manager, Amos Cornforth. Eleanor would not have entertained Clara's vain need for adoration, but Clara already knew she wouldn't get what she needed from the eldest twin, and did not waste her time.

Clara played with the children in the village, but this novelty soon wore thin. The children there were coarse, without fine clothes or beauty. They were either too in awe of her doll-like beauty to go anywhere near her, or they would mock her for her fine ways. She took to stealing eggs and would be found near the inn offering to tell people's fortunes in a broken egg in a bowl for a farthing. This wasn't appropriate for one of the most refined girls in the dale, and her antics soon caught the leery attentions of a couple of the men. Most wanted a woman, but there were always those who preferred the blonde, blue-eyed sweetness of a child.

Locals warned Maud and Ellen that they needed to take better care of the child. But Clara found ways of evading everyone put in charge of watching her. Eventually Old Marsden hobbled down to the inn and paid for her fortune, to see if there was anything in the nonsense she was mixing up in the yolks of eggs. Whether the old woman spotted a talent or not, no one could say, but she took the girl away and suggested she come visit the cottage every day instead. She'd teach her about herbs and healing. There were one or two regretful glances, but for now Clara remained untouched.

As long as the weather held Eleanor made regular trips over the moors to the edge of the world as she knew it. Sometimes she walked with Mary, sometimes with William when he was heading over to meet with his sweetheart. Occasionally she would find herself walking back with Megan of Osmotherley. Sisterly loyalty demanded that she hate the young woman and push her over a steep incline, for Eleanor truly felt her sister's pain. But she gradually opened up and accepted that Megan was indeed a good person. Even at the young age of twelve she knew that all was not fair in the world. Some days when she walked home alone, Atheleys would meet her part of the way. Despite the lack of any prearranged agreement, she somehow knew that Eleanor would be passing just then. The two girls would wander home through the sweet heather, chattering and laughing.

At Chequers Eleanor got to know Mrs Barker better, along with the Barker family and the set up of the farm. She'd entertain them with the different tunes she could play on her violin, and Mrs Barker would laugh and tell her she must be there in the spring when the drovers came through. They'd pay for the music, for the Scots loved their fast fiddle music, and Eleanor dreamed of all the shiny little coins she might gather, whilst surrounded by these strange exotic beasts: The Scots.

That Christmas the Hob, as Eleanor liked to think of her father – a habit picked up from her friend Atheleys and Mary Longbottom's childish jokes, spent a whole month in the family's company. At yuletide there were new shoes for all the children, a new dress and a ruby ring for Maud which became the object of envy for Clara. Clara received dresses and dolls and ribbons for her hair. Stephen little rag toys. And for the twins books, more specifically on the subjects of cookery and running a household. Hannah Glasse's wisdom went into the twins' hearts to varying degrees of success. Eleanor pretended to read the nuggets of domestic advice when she needed to quell the Hob's temper. In her mind she was daydreaming or composing fiddle jigs and reels. Gillian was devastated, for what wife would she ever be now that her darling had gone to another? It felt like the ultimate insult that she was to prepare for a future that would never be hers. At such a young age, the possibility that there might be more men had simply not entered her mind. She studied the book from cover to cover as a form of torture, constantly thinking of all the great touches to a home she could have offered to William. Megan of Osmotherley would never come up to her standards.

When the snows were at their worst, the family were grounded in Commondale. In the worst blizzards and clear days of snow drifts Clara did not even manage to get out to Old Marsden. The only person who would make any time for her was Gillian, but even then it was poor substitute for attention. Gillian only obsessed about her failings and how her life was over. She would have lamented at any willing audience, it was quite irrelevant that it was the porcelain doll Clara sat at the end of her bed. There was no joy to be had from Clara's angelic countenance. In a rather perverse chain of thoughts, Clara made the decision that winter that she was going to do Gillian a great favour. Although the details were yet to be worked out, Clara decided that she would arrange for Gillian's greatest desire, and in turn she would become an idol in Gillian's eyes.

As soon as it was possible to make the crossing over the moors to Chequers, Eleanor was on her feet, books and violin in a knapsack. She trekked over the wind-whipped, bleak moorland of the early year. Wrapped up in knitted woollens and thick skirts, she ploughed through blankets of snow and sheets of ice, often accompanied by a red-nosed Atheleys. People at either end of the journey were surprised she was so eager to try so early. Their concern did not stop them taking advantage however, and they would ask Eleanor to carry letters or goods back and forth. Chequers was close to the edge of the moors and the lowlands, where the postal services could get through a little easier. Mrs Barker, matriarchal head of Chequers, would stand, hands on hips and shake her head as she saw this young girl, only just creeping into womanhood, doing favours and earning the odd penny for the carrying of letters. All alone on the journey as far as she was aware, for Atheleys would never go past Black Hamilton. Something had to be done. She would find a way to ease the burden a little, and with that charitable thought in her mind, passed Eleanor a handful of letters and a wheel of cheese for a cousin in Commondale to take on her return journey.

It was when the snows were almost completely melted that Eleanor arrived one day to find a great change upon Chequers. From lonely inn and farmhouse, isolated up on the moors, it suddenly felt as though she was walking to a metropolis, or at least what a girl of such rural upbringing would imagine for city life. The place was bustling with far more souls than she had ever seen there. The surrounding fields were full of cattle, mooing and jostling and chewing the cud. Although she couldn't see Mrs Barker, she could hear her shrieking about the fine juicy green grass she'd been keeping for them. Horses were tied up at the front of the inn, heads in bags of oats, and a farmhand brushing down their sweaty coats. There was a group of geese honking in a pen. Dogs yapped and scampered around the yard. One of the dogs broke away from the pack, barking gleefully and running up to Eleanor, bounding up to put his front paws on her thighs as the two were reunited. "Wee Jamie!" she exclaimed, recognising the collie dog from last year. She gave his head a fuss, receiving licks and slobberings in return. "You've brought a few friends with you this time."

"You two have met before, then? I don't remember you, lassie, from the last time we were passing down here."

The accent was strong and very different to what they heard in this part of Yorkshire. But it was not so difficult to understand. Up at the inn leant a middle aged man against the low stone wall in front of the building. He had a great fuzzy beard and eyebrows that were ever reaching out from his face. He had a wide brimmed hat that would provide secondary shelter to his eyes from the rain after those eyebrows. A sprig of rowan was tucked into a band around the hat. He also wore a great overcoat, the long collar like a cape to his elbows and sturdy, mud splattered boots that had walked more miles than Eleanor could even imagine. He was fussing with a pipe as he engaged with the young Yorkshire lassie, getting the tobacco just right before he lit up. He looked back across at the girl from under his bushy eyebrows, awaiting some kind of response.

Eleanor stared at him in awe, this great exotic creature with the strange Scottish accent, with feet that had travelled the length of their island. What things he must have seen. What a life. Far more than roaming local moors, half-heartedly helping out with chores in the kitchen. Listening to the mindless chatter and gossip of people who had never been further than a day's walk. "You're from Scotland," she breathed, speaking the first thing that came into her mind.

He broke out into gruff laughter. "Aye, that'd be right. Was it the way I speak that gave it away?"

"You're not wearing tartan."

He gave her a long hard stare. "Don't they teach you anything down here in these southern lands? Or is this a trick?"

Her eyes widened in horror, feeling that she'd caused offense but not sure how. "No, I..."

Just a child, he reminded himself. An ignorant farm girl. "No one wears tartan these days. It's illegal. The government don't have a fondness for anything to do with the clans. Not after Culloden and all those troubles."

She was soaking up information, committing words and comments to memory. She'd have to try and find out what he was talking about later.

The dog was a little put out that he was no longer getting attention, and reinitiated his attack of barking and jumping up to Eleanor. "Jamie!" they both exclaimed, Eleanor laughing at the creature's glee, the man gruff and disapproving.

"He's a working dog, not a toy," he grumbled as he sent the dog a signal to go fetch his supper. "Far too spoiled."

"He's your dog?" she asked. She flicked through her memories of what Mrs Barker had told her of the drovers. "You're Mr MacCaskill. You're a drover."

"Correct on two counts. I am Cameron MacCaskill, and a drover I am, as this licence will show." He flourished a piece of paper from his pocket which Eleanor barely got a glimpse of before it was stowed away. "I don't like to get it damaged by the weather. I only wear it for the markets."

"But Jamie's not your dog?"

"He's part of the working pack here, along with the horses and the other men. But no, technically he's not my dog. He belongs to my nephew, Angus, who's away inside getting some food inside his belly." He considered the girl. Rather bold for one so young looking, and seemingly with no chores to be getting to. He had noted the knapsack she carried, as if she was a traveller or trader herself. "And might you be a girl from the village?"

"The village, yes," she started before realising not everyone knew the village to be Commondale. He was probably referring to Osmotherley down the hill. "Or rather I'm from a village. Not Osmotherley."

He laughed. "There's a great many villages in this region."

"I'm from Commondale. It's six hours walk that way." She waved vaguely with her arm.

"Aye, I know of Commondale," he said, although offered no more details onto how or why. "And what do you go by?"

Eleanor looked confused.

"Do you have a name, lass?"

"Oh, yes, Eleanor Hurst, sir," Automatically she did a little curtsey which set the drover off laughing again.

"Miss Hurst of Commondale," his laughter faltered as something occurred to him. "You're not at all related to that merchant, Hobart Hurst?"

"He's my father."

"Is he now?" A dark look crossed his face. "Well, you're not at all what I would have expected. And what are you doing away over here?"

"I have some letters for Mrs Barker." People from all over the valley were in the habit of passing letters and packages to her now that her walks had become common knowledge.

"Is that so? You'd best be away into the inn and see Mrs Barker about your business." He swept an arm out to invite her into the building as if he were the proprietor himself. Eleanor walked up and past him, though a light cloud of tobacco smoke.

Inside the inn was packed with people, Scottish drovers, workers at Chequers and locals up from Osmotherley to join in with the joviality and excitement of visitors. This was a time to catch up with news, get long distance favours and simply to soak up something more than the few miles of land surrounding one's humble abode. There was much talking and laughter, great tankards of beer, steaming plates of food and bowls of stew. Men were hunched around tables getting an update on world affairs, hearing tales of the American War of Independence that had started the year previous. Many felt it was a disgrace to fight against the King, George the third. The Scots were full of tales of recent years that would become legendary, knew what happened since the battle of Culloden and the end of the great Pretender. All wondered how it would go with the battles across the seas in the new world. Some had sons in the army who had been shipped over the oceans to play their role in defending the King's territories. Dispatches and letters were few and far between, and the drovers, who passed through all the major cities, were a news network in their own right. These men had started their journey up at the cattle markets at Falkirk and were eventually destined for London town. Eleanor felt giddy, drunk on glimpses of conversations of so many faraway places: London, Scotland, America. Just to imagine what a tiny speck upon the earth her homeland moors must be.

"Eleanor!" Mrs Barker cried out, catching sight of the girl as she laid out plates of food on a table. "I'm glad you're here today, and finally you'll meet our droving folk. You'll be playing us a few tunes, will you?"

"Musician, are you?" Cameron MacCaskill appeared behind her. "And what instrument would you be playing?"

"The fiddle."

"The fiddle, is it? I hope you're knowing some good jigs."

"Who's this fiddler of Yorkshire?" One of the Scots with a great dark beard eyed her up and down. "I've never the day seen this wee lass here before."

"This is Miss Eleanor Hurst," Mrs Barker put an arm around her shoulders. "The finest fiddler for many a mile, and a dear friend of mine, so you'll be minding your manners around her, Seamus."

He roared with laughter, "I'm nothing but manners, my fine woman. Happy to make your acquaintance, Miss Hurst of Osmotherley."

"I'm not from here."

"Oh?"

"She's from over Colmondale way," Mrs Barker explained.

"Colmondale? As in Commondale?"

"Yes, it's over..."

"Aye, I know the place," Cameron said. "I was there once; many a year ago now." He paused thoughtfully as he sucked on his pipe. "Hurst of Commondale, you say? You wouldn't be related to a certain merchant by the name of Mr Hobart Hurst?"

"He's my father."

That raised a few eyebrows round the gathering of drovers.

"Is he now? Well, you wouldn't know to look at you."

"I heard of a Hobart Hurst," a man further back in the room shouted. "A Hob Hurst, over Derbyshire way. Although he was no merchant. He was known for helping out the shoemaker." That comment brought out a wave of raucous laughter from his table, a private joke among friends perhaps. "I heard you could meet him on the moors."

For the first time Eleanor was hesitant, wondering if she really ought to be here. She didn't understand what they were talking about, although there appeared to be a common understanding about Hob Hurst. It didn't feel like the distant and ambivalent impression she had of her father. He spent so much time gone from home, what was she to know of who he actually was?

"Never you mind them," Mrs Barker said. "Nothing but drivel."

"Old wives tales."

"You come along here and get your fiddle set up."

Eleanor stared up at the woman. "Do you know what they're talking about?"

Mrs Barker looked a little uncomfortable as she led Eleanor to the back of the room. "Just old folktales from other parts. Not your father. It's mere chance that it's a similar name."

"So who is Hob Hurst?"

"No one for you to worry about."

She set Eleanor down at the end of a bench. "Now why don't you play us some music?"

"Hob Hurst, you say?" An unnoticed man sat further down the bench spoke up, making the two women jump. They looked to the rear of the inn where a young Scot was hunched over a bowl of stew. His hat was carelessly thrown upon the table, his overcoat hanging on a peg in the wall behind him. He carried an unkempt wild mop of red waves upon his head and a sharp twinkle in his eye. "He was a hobgoblin, wasn't he?"

"Angus MacCaskill," Mrs Barker snapped. "Never mind your nonsense."

"But it's the truth! I've heard the tale coming up through Derbyshire."

"That's enough," she continued, ignoring his wounded look, for he didn't understand what he had done wrong. "Now, this young lady is going to play us some music, so you mind yourself."

"I never do anything but."

Eleanor stared at him. "Angus MacCaskill."

"Aye, I am he," he said, a little uncertainly. He wasn't quite sure what these two women were about.

"Wee Jamie's your dog."

His face broadened out into a smile. "That he is. He's not been causing any trouble now?"

"No. I met him last year when he was going back to Scotland on his own."

"And he remembered you just the now?" He finished for her. "Oh, wee Jamie never forgets a face."

Eleanor put her knapsack down on the table and took out her fiddle and bow, carefully unwrapping the pieces from the rags she used to protect them whilst she was on the move. Setting the fiddle to her chin, she plucked at each string in turn, checking the sound. She doubted she managed to tune it perfectly, but with a few slight adjustments they sounded right enough. She ran the bow across the full range of strings to make sure that they hummed harmoniously. As Mrs Barker walked back into the fray, Eleanor started on a simple but pleasing tune Mr Meriwether had taught her. It blended into the background and was barely noticed. As she played on she grew embarrassed. Perhaps they were all hard of hearing from the long days out in all weather. Their sensibilities didn't extend to polite music played in the drawing rooms of civilised folk.

She came to the end of the tune and sat down. She was a child. Mrs Barker was always impressed with anything she played, but that was when there weren't many folk at Chequers and people didn't have such exciting news to catch up with.

Angus coughed awkwardly. "That was very proficient," he offered.

"It was boring."

"Aye, well..." his gaze wandered off into the clusters of his drover companions in the inn. "You don't know anything a bit more... lively, do you?"

Not from the book of music for young ladies. Those kinds of tunes only asked for the subdued and polite clapping at the end of the performance. But there were the unwritten tunes she had committed to memory: the ones Atheleys had taught her. They were faster, jumping, and it was barely all she could do to keep up with herself. Whoever had originally written those tunes must have lived their life in a whirl. Eleanor started to tap out the rhythm with her foot, pondering over which one to open with. Lifting up the bow, she started again, this time with a refrain that would speed up and increase with intensity as the reel went on. It was one of those that could naturally flow into a whole catalogue of other melodies from Atheleys.

Something in this rhythm spoke to the drovers, and foot taps soon accompanied her music, along with appreciative nodding and a bit of clapping, before it broke out into joyful yipping. A couple of the men jumped up to swing Mrs Barker and one of the serving girls around the room. Just beside her at the table Angus marked time with hand drumming on the table top. As she went into another reel Eleanor was a little in awe just how much this music resonated with the Scots. She wondered if Atheleys wasn't Scottish. She really knew precious little about the girl.

Beads of sweat glistened on her forehead as she rolled into the crescendo before coming to a break. Her arms needed a couple of minutes to rest before she started again. One of the Scots raised his tankard to her in passing. "You been learning your music from the trowies, lassie?"

"She's Hob Hurst's daughter, don't you know?" someone shouted from within the crowds.

"Oh aye, that'll explain it."

Eleanor looked confused. "Trowie?" she whispered as the man wandered off.

"Don't mind Big James," Angus told her. "He's from Shetland, islands to the far north. They're a funny folk up there. Trowies are their little people."

"Children?"

He smiled wryly. "No, you ken what I mean. You have them round here, but you call them hobgoblins. Trowies are known for sitting on their mounds and playing the fiddle."

"Oh." Well, it had been music from Atheleys.

Angus gestured to her fiddle that rested upon the table. "May I?"

"You play?"

"A little," he admitted as he flexed his fingers before picking up the fiddle. "I'm guessing you have a memory for the tunes, yes? I'll play you a few from the land where I hail from. You can practice them for next time we're coming through." He gave her a wink.

Eleanor watched in amazement as the young man nimbly started up on a fast reel. He had a sharper, almost stabbing like action with the bow, certainly different to the gentle waves she tended to cast across the strings. The notes came out clear and bounding. Music of faraway lands. She concentrated on the rhythm, the pattern of notes, and humming along as she picked up on the melody, so desperate to remember every bit. She would practice this incessantly until it was engraved upon her very soul. When he was finished, and passed her back the fiddle, there was a slight smell of him about it. She practiced through the first reel, being corrected by Angus here and there when she misremembered the odd section. Soon she was up to speed, with people clapping along and Angus laughing in delight that she had learned one of his people's songs so quickly.

Eleanor swore loudly and loosened her grip on the rope. The palms of her hands were burning red. She had pulled as much as she could. For her thirteen years she felt she had more strength than many girls of the same age, but this was too much. It was all to no avail. Huffing, she took a fresh grip on the rope, preparing herself for another attempt. She was surprised they had managed to travel these five miles already, but the good pace had been shattered and at this rate they would never get home. She glared at the donkey. The beast looked blankly at her in return. She focused her stare, hoping the message would get through the donkey's thick skull. They needed to move.

She pulled hard and the donkey set its legs rigid in position. Eleanor let out a wail and the donkey started to bray, victorious and stubborn. They were going nowhere. Eleanor dropped the rope and the donkey took a couple of steps to the side of the path. Drawing back its lips it started to cautiously nibble on a thistle.

"I never wanted a donkey," Eleanor complained. "What did I do to deserve you?"

The donkey rudely ignored her and continued nibbling at the greenery to the side of the path.

This had been Mrs Barker's idea of helping with Eleanor's situation in life. Unintentionally she had caused more trouble than help. The idea had been that Eleanor would be able to transport more than just letters between Osmotherley and Commondale during her travels back and forth. Make a little money, make the trips pay for themselves. It would save her having to carry everything, and also make it possible to accept weightier parcels. That had been the idea. Apparently there had been some money gathered last night in appreciation of her fiddle skills. The money had somehow disappeared into the finances of the inn on this occasion, Eleanor not seeing so much as a ha'penny. But she had been given a donkey that was to set her up in a little business of her own.

It was a nice idea, but Eleanor was thinking she would have rather taken the money. Not that she had been given a choice. What good was this donkey to her? She was considering walking away, for she wanted to be home again, but she could hardly abandon her earnings in this way. "Perhaps I should chop you up and turn you into stew," she threatened.

The donkey merely curled its lip and looked ready to break in to a scornful laugh.

"This is hopeless!" She yelled, kicking at a rock and shouting even more when the rock she thought had been loose was actually firmly embedded in the ground. It proved harsh resistance to her kick.

A childish giggle behind alerted her to Atheleys' presence.

Wiping with the back of her hand at the tears that had sprung in her eyes, she turned around to see Atheleys loitering further up the path. She was an odd character. Dressed in the same clothes as the day they had first met, and yet grown to the same height as Eleanor. Those clothes ought to have been stretched out to broken rags, yet they still fit perfectly.

"What are you doing shouting at rocks and donkeys?"

"It won't move."

"The rock?"

"No, silly," Eleanor rolled her eyes, then broke out into a smile, her fury abating. "The donkey. Mrs Barker gave it to me as she thought I could make a business. Transporting things on the donkey. But it won't move. I ought to be a few miles further up the path by now."

"I know. I was waiting for you." Atheleys casually folded her arms behind her back and strolled down the path towards Eleanor. "Shall I talk to your donkey? Donkeys like me."

"I don't think this one likes anyone."

"What's her name?"

"I don't know. Mrs Barker didn't say." Eleanor paused. "How do you know it's a she?"

"It's obvious, isn't it? Let's call her Assa," Atheleys decided as she walked up to the beast. As she stepped up to the grey, fluffy creature, the donkey stopped eating and swung its head around to look at the silver haired child. Atheleys put her hand on Assa's forehead between her eyes. "There now. Why do you want to be so awkward? Don't you know Miss Hurst will take good care of you?"

"You think Assa's going to respond to logic?"

Atheleys grinned and looked over at her. "You're calling her by her name at least. Come on, let's go." She leant forward to pick up the slack rope and offered it to Eleanor.

Eleanor was not convinced. "Just like that?"

"Just like that. Come on, we've got a long way to go yet before we're home."

Eleanor remained still on the path as Atheleys started walking back up the slope. She looked from her friend's back to Assa, who stood blinking. This wasn't going to work. Determined, she tightened her grip around the rope in both hands and took a few steps forward to get the rope taught and ready to pull. Assa sniffed and started to follow without protest. She looked back at the donkey in disbelief. Just like that. It was a fluke. Give it half an hour and the beast would be braying and pulling to a stop.

"Are you coming, Eleanor?" Atheleys shouted back over her shoulder. "We haven't got all day."

Megan of Osmotherley sometimes wondered to herself if one person ought to have so much happiness. Could it be possible for life to be this blissful? Those were her thoughts on some occasions, but she would remind herself that things were not perfect, for the bliss was being delayed. William would not wed her until he had saved up enough money. She had said on countless occasions that it didn't matter, but William could be very single minded, and would not be swayed from his path. Still, it was no matter. The time for their wedding would come around soon enough.

It was a hot summer. One could almost hear the heat crackling at the dry bracken through the stillness. The heather was on the brink of blooming. In a few more weeks the hills would turn a glorious purple, and the sweet scent of heather blossom would be carried on the moorland breezes.

It was late afternoon and Megan had set back on her trek to Osmotherley. William had intended on walking with her, but a horse had lost a shoe and the rider was adamant it was to be fixed as soon as possible. They couldn't turn down any money, so eager they were to build up that nest egg. Megan had assured him she was quite capable of walking home alone, and shouldered her bag. There was a lucky horseshoe in the bottom that William had given her as a love token that day. She would hang it where she slept when she returned home. William's mother had given her a cloth bundle with bread and cheese. She'd eat that on the high rocks in the late summer sun at the Wainstones. In fact, she could quite happily eat the food now but she still had such a long way to go.

She had not yet even reached Baysdale, and was traversing the moorland hills between the two valleys.

Like a tease, the scent of cooking twisted into her nostrils. It smelt as though someone had a fine stew on the boil. It wasn't often anyone was seen cooking on top of the moors. Most people travelling over here knew the network of tiny villages and farms scattered across the moors and could soon get themselves to an inn or the fireside of acquaintances fairly quickly. Occasionally there'd be traveller folk, although they wouldn't usually drag horses and caravans this high. The drovers cut across other sections of the high moors to get to York and London far beyond. Anything to avoid a toll road. Drovers and travellers made Megan nervous. Their worldly ways, and knowledge of the greater country made her feel small and inadequately homely. And that they saw her as a simpleton to be taken advantage of. People all said the drovers were to be trusted, men of honour, for not any man could get a droving licence. The gypsies were different, secluded in their strange languages and symbols and seemingly mystical understanding.

She saw the curl of smoke from a camp fire close to a lonely copse of trees. Normally Megan would have avoided any other travellers on the paths, one never knew if it might be a highway man about his business, or some equally corrupt man looking for fresh victims. As the path neared, she saw movement and realised there was only one figure at the cooking pot. Not only that, but it was a child. A little girl with long golden curls. She wore a neat dress and pinafore, and stirred at a little cooking pot over a fire as if she were playing at keeping house.

"Clara Hurst?" she exclaimed as she recognised the angelic little girl.

Clara looked up and waved shyly, a sweet smile on her lips.

"Clara Hurst, what are you doing out here alone on the moors?" Megan left the track and waded through the heather to Clara's camp. The child was only but seven and shouldn't be away so far from home, and in such a remote place.

"Cooking my supper," Clara said, as if every young child took it upon itself to walk miles into the wilderness to boil up a stew.

"I can see that. It certainly smells very good. But why aren't you at home?"

"Children should be out in the sun in summer. I get under Mama's feet. She's busy with the baby." Clara swallowed down anger at the usurper, keeping her expression sweet for Megan's benefit. Baby Stephen, now a one year old toddler, made her furious every day. People would coo and clap at whatever he did, and mostly he was an imbecile. Clara was ignored more and more. Gillian was a shadowy wraith, either working at her chores or studying the bible, but always with her eyes down and little to say. Eleanor was increasingly off running errands with that horrible donkey that just kicked and brayed whenever Clara went anywhere near it. She hadn't liked the creature the day Eleanor had brought it home. Mama had been horrified, for how would they pay for the feed, but Eleanor's predictions had soon proved right that the money she earned from her errands would keep Assa. Assa: what a stupid name for a donkey. And what a stupid donkey it was. It had different levels of tolerance for people living at Pines Lodge, but as a general rule did exactly what it pleased unless Eleanor was there.

Megan set her bag in the heather and knelt by the cooking pot. The stew did smell very good. She'd heard that Old Marsden had taken Clara under her wing and was teaching her about herbs and spices. Clearly something was working as the mere scent of this concoction set her stomach rumbling. She stirred the pot with the wooden spoon, noting the pieces of meat. "What type of stew is it?"

"Rabbit."

"Rabbit? How did you get a rabbit?" She glanced up at Clara and caught a guilty look on her face. "You've not been poaching, have you?"

"It was dead in a trap when I found it."

"Ah well, I don't suppose anyone's going to miss one little rabbit." And who would believe that such a sweet little child would have taken it either?

"Will you not share my stew with me?" Clara burst out. "I've made too much and you'll be walking all the way back to Osmotherley, won't you? You've still a long way to go."

Megan hesitated. She had wanted to be further on than this before she stopped to eat, but this stew was very tempting.

"I have two little bowls," Clara offered.

"I have some bread we could have with the stew," Megan added, and it was decided. Stew it would be.

So they sat together, woman and child, and ate up the stew and bread to their satisfaction. The cooking pot was not so large, so they easily cleaned the pot without feeling too bloated afterwards. In fact, Megan felt particularly energised with the meal, and eager to start walking again, as if her legs could not bear to be still. She thanked Clara again for the meal, happy over the chance meeting and the pleasant company. Shouldering her bag, she set off again on her way home.

Clara sat and watched Megan on her way until she was just a mere dot in the distance. She took a small brown glass bottle out of her pinafore pocket and pulled out the stopper. She gulped the contents in one go, popping the stopper back in and slipping the bottle back out of sight. The reaction was quick, and in a couple of minutes the concoction had started to work. Clara was on all fours, retching into a pre dug hole between two heather shrubs. Tears streamed from her eyes as she vomited, the undigested stew of rabbit and various vegetables spewing out into the dry, dusty earth. When she was finished, she rested for some time, lying back in the heather and staring up at the blue sky. She then took one of the little bowls and used it to shovel dirt back in over the hole. She poured a pot of water on the remaining fire, then scooped more earth to cover over it. Bundling up the pots and metal rods that formed the cooking frame, Clara slung her lightweight little supper set over her shoulder and set off for home.

Megan had been down to Baysdale and was back up on the moors following the curve of land around to the Wainstones when she first started to feel strange. Her body felt light, almost insubstantial, and her vision flickered. Perhaps she had taken too much sun. This section of the track followed the edge of quite a steep drop. She kept her eyes on the path and her feet to make sure she didn't take a false step. The path loomed up at her as if it were alive. Strange colours and shapes moved before her. Something fast and small ran out across the path as if to jump at her. Frightened, Megan cried out and stumbled backwards as if a creature was trying to bite at her feet. She lost her balance and tripped off the path, stumbling through tall dry grass before the earth disappeared and she went tumbling down the incline, rocks and the contents of her bag striking her as she went.

It wasn't until the following day, just after midday, that anyone realised what had happened. Megan's own people hadn't been certain which day she would return, and so did not worry when she was not home that evening. Likewise the Longbottoms assumed she was safely in her bed in Osmotherley as they retired for the night.

In an odd twist, it was Eleanor Hurst who discovered the young woman. Eleanor had been across at Chequers and was making her way back to Commondale, with her faithful donkey Assa. It was as they were crossing the moors heading towards the dale where Baysdale Abbey sat, that Eleanor first heard the moaning. Not giving it much thought, she continued on her route, until she heard the sounds again, a half-heard thought that there may have been human words jumbled in the sound. She stopped walking abruptly, Assa not paying attention and bumping into her shoulder with her hot muzzle. The donkey shook its head in irritation and looked down the steep slope. As the earth crept towards the valleys, fissures would open up, where the heather broke apart and thick, scrubby grass, bracken and woody birch trees emerged from the ground, hiding an arsenal of jagged rocks.

Eleanor looked at Assa for confirmation of the sound, but Assa said nothing, as was her habit. She looked up the path, then back the way they had come. There were no other travellers.

"Is anyone there?"

A weak cry echoed up from the bottom of the slope.

Oh god, Eleanor thought. There was someone down there. Perhaps they had fallen, or maybe a highway man had taken them, dragging them down into the shadows and beating them senseless before making off with their purse. This could be a trap. She loitered indecisively. Assa's lead hung loose in her hands. What to do? She looked at her donkey. "Wait here," she whispered, looping the lead around Assa's shoulders.

Taking a stout walking stick out of Assa's saddle packs, Eleanor tentatively stepped off the path and with the boldness of the young, started down the slope. She jabbed her walking stick into the earth with every step, grabbing handfuls of dried grass now and then when she felt as though she was about to lose her balance "Are you hurt?" she called out. She only received mumbles in return, but it was enough to direct her to the bottom of the dell.

As she neared, she saw the broken fronds of bracken, and an uncontrolled pathway bashed down the side of the hill, where someone must have fallen. Ahead there was a tumble of rags and a human body encased within. Heavy skirts and long hair. A woman. Hair matted with blood. Dirty arms reached feebly upwards as they realised help was coming.

Eleanor held her breath as she recognised Megan of Osmotherley. What had she been doing? Megan knew these paths better than Eleanor, and she was quite sure she hadn't been drunk and sneaking about at midnight.

"Megan," she hurried up to the injured woman as she was now on relatively level ground at the bottom. "What happened? Were you attacked?"

Megan groaned, shuffling uncomfortably on the ground, but seemingly unable to sit up. Eleanor loomed into her view of the blinding sky, a sudden appearance of concern and youth. Megan squinted at her. "Gillian," she breathed. "So good to see you."

Eleanor pursed her lips. They were twins, identical twins at that, but in the last few months it seemed as though they were becoming very different creatures. Eleanor was actually growing faster and now had a couple of inches on her sister. She had a more robust, healthy look, and her skin was quite tanned from all the time she spent outdoors. She often forgot her bonnet, and her long dark hair would blow lose and get tangled most days. Gillian on the other hand was scrawny, wan and miserable, with a haunted look and her hair hidden beneath caps and bonnets as if she had some terrible affliction to hide.

"It's Eleanor," she told Megan, thinking the woman ought to be glad. If it was Gillian here, and god only knew what reason Gillian would have had for walking this path, she would have barely had the strength to help Megan, and certainly not the inclination. Eleanor crouched down beside her, quickly scanning over the ripped dress, scrapes and cuts on her forearms and the heavy wound to her head. "You've been attacked?"

"I fell," Megan whispered. "I felt strange."

"This whole thing is very strange," Eleanor muttered under her breath. "We have to get you out of here. Can you get up?" She helped Megan up to a sitting position, the woman yelping with pain as she put pressure on her right hip. This was not good. "Look, put your arm around my shoulders. We have to get back up to the path."

It was a great struggle, Assa stood at the top of the slope watching on with bewilderment as she chewed on a clump of heather without much satisfaction. It seemed that Megan's right leg would not work, and she could only weakly bent her left leg to give any kind of upward thrust as the girls virtually slithered their way up the bank. Sweat poured in rivulets down Eleanor's face and neck as she bore the brunt of the exertion and weight, disconcerted to listen to Megan sob in pain. She felt inept as she forced the woman upwards, worried she could be causing more damage than aid, but she did not know what else to do.

As they reached the top, they collapsed onto the path, gasping for breath as if they had just escaped from a raging sea. Eleanor, huddled on all fours, looked over at Megan. The woman was lying on her left side and shaking in pain. They were a long way from Osmotherley. She wasn't up to walking even a few steps, but Eleanor didn't want to run off and leave her here. They were much closer to Commondale, but even that was quite a walk, going down into the dale, back up onto the moors before crossing down to her home territory. The closest place was Baysdale Abbey, just down in the valley from here. They would have to head for that farm. It was called an Abbey, but only a farm holding now, surrounded by forest and green arable fields. There was a small river and an ancient bridge. Eleanor had heard that there had once been nuns somewhere there, although it had been called Basedale in those days, and of course the nunneries and monasteries were long gone these past two hundred years.

"Assa, can you carry her to the next farm?" She led the beast up to Megan. She touched Megan's shoulder. "We have to go to the next farm. You can ride on Assa."

"I can't sit, for it hurts too much," Megan wailed.

After some manoeuvring, they managed to get Megan onto Assa. It was a hopeless and unladylike position, lying on her belly over Assa's back. Her legs kicked the saddle bag on one side, her arms the other. But Megan said it was the least uncomfortable. It would have to do. Eleanor was keen to get to a farm where the farmer's wife would be able to take over and know what to do, as all adult women would.

The journey took longer than usual as Eleanor did not want to knock Megan too much. Every jolt as Assa walked sent fresh sobs though Megan. At some point she wavered in and out of consciousness and began to shiver despite the summer heat. Eleanor threw her shawl over the wounded woman, and felt intense relief when the farm buildings of Baysdale Abbey came into view.

A farm boy was the first to see Eleanor and her bizarre cargo approach the property. He ran inside, and soon reappeared with the farmer's wife. "Why, Miss Hurst," the woman called out, for Eleanor took letters to and from the property on her travels. "What's that you've got with you there?"

"It's Megan Hammond, of Osmotherley," she explained. "I found her off the path, up on the moors. It looked like she'd taken a tumble, and she's awful hurt. I didn't know what else to do." She felt tears prick at her eyes.

The woman hurried up to them, lifting up Megan's head. The girl wasn't with it, her eyes rolled back in her head and her forehead was chilled with sweat. Her hair was blood-matted. The woman noted the torn skirts. "What happened to her? Attacked?" she asked quietly. It had been a while since they'd had vagabonds and trouble on the moors.

Eleanor shook her head. "She said not."

"Aye, well, she's in a bad way, whatever the reason. We'd best get her in."

"She can't stand to use her left leg," Eleanor told her, as she went to grab Megan round the waist and pull her from the donkey.

"All right, you take her legs and we'll get her inside." She looked over at the farm boy. "And you, my lad, away down to Kildale now and fetch the doctor back here."

The farm lad gave a slight nod before scarpering off down the farm track.

They carried Megan into the farmhouse and manoeuvred her onto a little bed. A scullery maid appeared with a bowl of water and clean rags. Eleanor watched her set the items on a side table, having instinctively known what her mistress would ask for. The maid must have been Eleanor's age, if that. This girl was not doing household chores to help her own family, on occasion when she felt like it, but rather for backbreaking hours for a pittance of a wage. How lucky and how spoilt Eleanor must have seemed, being able to travel back and forth to Chequers on a whim, having had the time to run around and explore the moors. Some folk would have said it was because Eleanor was a better breed of person, and therefore she was able to enjoy an improved life, just as there were superior families to her own, where they lived in great mansions, dressed in silk and had an army of staff to care for their every need. Was it actually that one person was better than another, or was it merely random chance where one happened to be born? The little maid smiled shyly at Eleanor before scurrying out of the room.

Megan cried out in pain as she writhed in the bed. The older woman started to wipe away the dried blood from the girl's face. "My god, she's burning up," she gasped.

"But she's shivering."

"How long was she out there?"

"I don't know. She hasn't been able to say a lot to me."

"Well, it's a lucky thing you were passing when you were and heard her," the farmer's wife decided. "Or else this could have started off as a tragedy."

Eleanor's eyes widened slightly and she felt sick. Megan dead? She hadn't come across death that much. Oh, certainly with the sheep and the wild creatures of the moors, and there was always a sickness that would run through the little villages and take some of the younger and weaker children. But the fit children, the ones that grew up; they weren't supposed to die. At least as far as she had ever considered the subject.

Two hours after Eleanor had struggled her way down to the farmhouse, the doctor from the nearby village of Kildale was in the room with the farmer's wife, Mrs Gray, and the patient. Eleanor sat at the kitchen table with a bowl of untouched stew in front of her. She had lost her appetite. She didn't know quite what to do with herself. There was nothing more she could do for Megan and yet she felt that she ought to stay. She was worried that the screams from the little room had stopped. One might have wondered if the pain had ceased. A blessing perhaps, although for the observer whilst Megan was moaning and screaming, one could at least be sure that she was still in the land of the living.

Mrs Gray appeared in the kitchen. She looked drawn. "He's bleeding her."

"She'd already lost a lot of blood from the fall."

She gave Eleanor a sharp look. "I'm sure the doctor knows what he's doing."

Eleanor lowered her eyes to the stew.

Mrs Gray relented and sat down at the table opposite the young girl. She petted her hand. "You have nothing to worry about. You did the right thing. You got her up and away and straight to the nearest place of help. If she'd been left out there for another night, for the doctor thinks she's already been out one, she would most certainly have died, and then you would have been bringing a different cargo to me."

Eleanor felt her lip wobble and wiped at her eyes.

"The doctor says she's not to be moved, so she'll stay with us for now. I know her mother." She looked gravely out the window. There were maybe three to four hours of light left, but probably not enough to get over to Osmotherley today. "I'll send word first thing in the morning. What about her betrothed? Doesn't he live in Commondale?"

Eleanor nodded weakly. Dear besotted William. "I'll go home today and let him know."

"Aye." She folded her hands together. "First you'll eat that stew and wait to hear what the doctor has to say before you go. Best to have as many details as you can, for he'll only be asking you questions."

A door opened and the doctor walked out, wiping his hands on a cloth. He gestured back towards the room. "There's a bowl there that needs emptying."

Mrs Gray nodded. "I'll get Milly on it."

He returned to the room, and shortly left again, this time with his bag, hat and coat. He came into the kitchen and set the items on the table to ready himself for the journey back home. "I've bled her now, but she's lost in a fever. She's delirious. There are a lot of cuts from the fall, and it feels as though her hip has been crushed. There is nothing I can do for this, we must keep her as still as we can and hope that nature can help. But Mrs Gray, it's important you watch her overnight. Keep her brow wetted and keep her wrapped up in blankets. She must sweat out this fever and I fear it will reach its peak tonight. If she does not beat it..." he paused, catching sight of Eleanor's grey face. "You, my child, have nothing to reproach yourself for. You have given this young woman the best chance for finding her after this accident." He looked back to Mrs Gray. "I believe you said there is a fiancé over in Commondale?"

"Yes, he's from the same place as Miss Hurst here."

"I would suggest he is told as soon as possible. He may wish to get here with some urgency in case..." he let the rest of his reasoning hang unspoken. Everyone understood the implications.

Mrs Gray thumped a heavy fist on the table. "Alan!" she roared.

There was a crashing sound outside of something being knocked over, then the farm boy Eleanor had first seen on approach to the farm appeared in the doorway.

"Is that donkey fed and watered?"

"Yes, Mrs. It's out in the stable."

Eleanor put a few spoonfuls of stew into her mouth. "I should go," she said, getting up from the table. "I'll get word to William."

Assa was a little disgruntled that she was to be pulled out from her stabling and hay so quickly, but begrudgingly accepted and only brayed once when Eleanor hopped up onto her back. They needed to get home quickly, and they'd go faster on Assa's four sturdy little legs. The two of them clattered out of the farmyard, past the doctor's horse, and away on the track past green fields and good farming before the next incline up to the moorland tops, and the final upland stretch before they would wind down into Commondale.

It was the quickest Eleanor had ever crossed those miles yet it felt as though it took the longest of ages. The track came out at the top end of the village, where her own home stood. She could feel that Assa was tired, and didn't want to drag the creature about anymore. She went home first, putting Assa to rest in the stables and hurrying into the house with the saddlebags to fling them into her room and out of the way. Ellen Withers was sitting outside of the house with Maud and Clara, plaiting corn dollies. They looked up in surprise when Eleanor rushed past and asked what the matter was, but Eleanor didn't have time to answer.

Gillian was in the room that they shared, studying her bible. She looked up in disinterest as Eleanor slung the bags onto the bed, but paid a little more attention when she noted Eleanor's dishevelled and distressed appearance.

"What's happened?"

"Megan Hammond's been in a terrible accident. She might not make it through the night. I have to get William."

Gillian stared blankly at her for a moment. Then her face fell apart and she started to scream. She slammed the bible shut and flung it at the wall.

"Give over, Gillian. It's not you that's dying."

Gillian roared at her.

Eleanor hurried out of the room. She didn't have time for her sister's mixed emotions. In the kitchen she met with Clara, who was just retreating inside with a half-finished corn dolly. She smiled sweetly at Eleanor. "Is she dead yet?"

"No," Eleanor muttered distractedly, brushing past her. "She's just having a tantrum."

Baby Stephen started to cry as the crashing noise from the twin's room woke him up. Maud ran into the house to go to her distressed child. "Gillian, stop that hullaballoo at once!" she shouted.

Eleanor hurried out, past Ellen Withers who was now alone with the straw. "My, Eleanor. It was lovely and peaceful until you got back," she joked.

"I have to go to the Longbottom's," Eleanor called over her shoulder as she ran down towards the village. It was only when she was rushing up to the Longbottom house and hammering on the door that she realised Clara hadn't been asking about Gillian. But then the door was opened by Mr Longbottom, and she forgot all about her little sister, in the hurry to get her message passed onwards to William.

The fever did not take Megan that night. At some point in the small hours of the morning the sweat broke and the danger passed. She was lethargic and weak for weeks afterwards. Although she had survived the fever, she did not come out of the episode unscathed. The doctor had been correct that she had severely damaged her hip. Megan could not move in the bed due to agonising shooting pains. During her confinement her body blistered out with bed sores for her suffering, which had to be treated once her hip had taken weeks to heal enough to allow movement.

William abandoned his work and spent his time at Baysdale Abbey. He worked on the farm to pay for the board and lodging Mrs Gray kindly offered, and was at Megan's bedside holding vigil and praying to God in every other waking hour. Megan was certain she was going to die, and told William to leave her. He assured her he would never abandon her under any circumstance, although little did either of them know that those were words he would come to deeply regret.

When Gillian had first heard the news of Megan's accident, she had exploded in blind fury. After a night lying in bed, seething at darkness, she had been so confused that she did not know what to do or think. She was devastated for Megan, as any good Christian girl would be, and for William and the shattering of all his plans. But there was also a demon inside that laughed gleefully. For if Megan died, William could become hers. She became terrified that others may realise her dark thoughts, and felt guilty, as if she had been out on the moors and pushed Megan over the precipice. This guilt became a chain around her soul when Clara started to beg for praise and attention, claiming that this was all her work that she had arranged for Gillian's benefit. Gillian had slapped her and called her an evil little witch. Clara had burst into tears, claiming that this was what Gillian had wished for and she had only been following her sister's will. Gillian didn't really believe Clara had any power, or anything to do with what had been an unfortunate accident. But the guilt gnawed at her, until she thought she might die. Clara turned cold on her that day, and ever after she couldn't help but wonder if Clara wished her ill and cursed what had meant to be a gift. By the end of the week they knew that Megan would survive.

As the damage healed Megan was able to walk again, but it would never be the same. She had a shuffling gait, a dreadful limping hobble that was worse than Ellen Wither's movement. She was intensely grateful for the return of mobility, but it was obvious from the awkward way the hip had misformed that she was never going to walk great distances. What came as a harder blow was the doctor's final verdict that although Megan would live, grow in strength, and only suffer from aches in her hips in the cold and damp, the internal damage had been great, and she would never bear children. For Megan, the only purpose of a woman was to set up home and provide offspring for her husband. She was devastated by the news and couldn't see William. She arranged transport on a cart and fled back to her family home in Osmotherley, refusing to see anyone for several weeks.

Around that time that Gillian started flagellating herself.

It was strange how one event seemed to have so many repercussions, Eleanor reflected as she gazed down at Pines Lodge. Megan Hammond had little to do with their household beyond blocking Gillian's unrequited love. And yet so many dynamics had changed since the day of that accident. Gillian had become nervous and pious, constantly looking for ways to punish herself as if she had done something she needed to atone for. She seemed to be almost terrified of Clara. Clara remained her usual vain self with everyone, but Eleanor had watched when Gillian and Clara thought they were alone. Clara looked down on Gillian as if she were a wretch. And an ungrateful wretch at that. Clara's question from the night Eleanor had returned to Commondale after finding Megan still disturbed her. Eleanor was convinced that Clara had known something about the accident, and perhaps it was that knowledge that gave her power over Gillian. She hoped to all that was sacred that Gillian hadn't done something stupid. Gillian was so religious, and so keen to do the Christian thing, she hoped that her fervour would have kept her from doing anything rash in jealousy.

She watched as her mother, carrying little Stephen, wandered across the yard to where Amos stood. Little players upon a stage. Why was she so familiar with the land manager? Did she not hear some of the whispers that had already started in the village? Eleanor was young and naive but she knew love when she saw it, even in a parent, who, as all children knew, ought to be long past the times of desire and love. The stupid things people did for love, Eleanor thought scornfully. She'd never make any foolish mistakes.

Flopping back into the heather, she flicked through her new book. Her eyes scanned over the flurry of notes marked onto the pages. There were a lot of good tunes to learn from this book, and it would certainly keep her occupied over winter. She fully intended to learn them all by heart, and then next spring she'd be able to impress the drovers with her repertoire.

She closed the book and ran a hand over the cover. Traditional music of Scotland. Angus MacCaskill had turned up with wee Jamie at Chequers this late autumn, on his way back to Scotland. He'd said that he had decided to save more of his money, and was therefore going back home by foot rather than riding by carriage as many of the other drovers chose to do. It had been good to see the land he'd travelled through touched by autumn; such vibrant colours, he'd said. Wee Jamie had been glad of the company, even if it would probably take him twice as long to get back to his place by the fireside this year. And that evening at the inn, Angus had given Eleanor this book of music. Something he'd picked up in London, as he thought she might want to learn a few more tunes. There was only so much one man who was just passing through could teach her.

Tucking the book under her arm, she wandered down through the heather towards home. When she arrived at the farmstead her mother and Amos were swinging Stephen up and down between the two of them, the child shrieking with delight. Hobart Hurst hadn't been to the farm for weeks, if not months now. As the years went by he seemed to spend less and less time at the property. Almost as if it were a mere lodging house for him. Eleanor sometimes wondered if he had another family, and another household somewhere else in the country that suited him better. Or perhaps he was out living in the hills, as those old Scottish drovers had suggested.

In the kitchen Ellen Withers was swearing at the fire as she lobbed another turf onto the smouldering pile. Despite all the years she'd been here, she'd never gotten completely used to the local habit of burning turfs, and still much preferred firewood and logs. She stabbed at the fire with an iron poker. "Damn fire," she muttered. "You've not been out since I moved here. You will not beat me."

"You just need a bit of kindling in there." Eleanor took a handful out of the basket and crouched down by the fireplace. Shifting a couple of turfs, for Ellen had overloaded the fire, she found a few glowing embers and got them sparking again.

The fire salvaged, she stood up and brushed her hands on her skirts.

"Miss Eleanor Hurst!" Ellen scolded with a smile on her mouth. "You'll not make a fine lady like that." She considered the slightly awkward girl. "Why, you're almost the same height as me. When did you shoot up like that? How old are you now?"

"Thirteen."

"Thirteen. My god. I remember the time here before you even existed."

Eleanor shuffled away to stand by the support posts near the chimney place. Ellen was getting increasingly nostalgic, as if she were an old woman, although Eleanor was sure she was no older than mama. Only just past thirty. And still here as a serving woman in the farmhouse. Never a marriage proposal, or certainly nothing the girls had heard about. And she'd never left, although no doubt she could have gone to one of the annual hirings and negotiated herself higher wages elsewhere. Eleanor wondered about the complexities of people's lives. Did they know how things would work out, or did they all start out where she was now? Leaning against the post, she ran her fingers in the old familiar groves of the pattern that had been carved into the post for as long as she could remember.

She stepped back and looked at the post. "When did this carving get done?"

Ellen gave it a cursory glance. "That's always been there."

"What's it for?"

"How should I know? These Yorkshire folk round here, they have some funny ideas." She broke off as she put a warming pan onto the range. "Mr Cornforth's people used to live here before us. Ask him if you want to know."

Eleanor scampered back out of the house. Hanging out of the front door, she called out to Mr Cornforth, or Amos as she'd always known him. "Amos!"

He looked up from swinging Stephen about but didn't stop the game.

"What are the carvings for?"

"What carvings, lass?"

"In the post, by the fire."

"Those. They've always been there." He shrugged, not particularly concerned, and far more distracted by the son he could not acknowledge publicly. "Ever since I was a lad. I think my grandmother said something about good luck."

Good luck didn't sound so exciting. "Oh."

As usual, she got a better explanation the next time she saw Atheleys. The two girls were sitting on a cairn, kicking their heels in the dry autumn earth and chattering about nothing in particular. Eleanor started telling her about the carved pattern on the post, which Atheleys was then able to draw out in the earth with her fingers. "It's to protect the home against witches," Atheleys told her before looking up with an amused grin on her face. "Although I don't think it's working there these days."

It was the first of July 1777, a Tuesday and the property at Pines Lodge was buzzing with people. It was the same every year with the clippings. The daytal men, at least forty of them, had descended on Commondale yesterday evening, and had been up at the crack of dawn. They'd make good money, but they'd work hard for it. The entire sheep holdings of Hobart Hurst, which had grown to a mighty size over the years were to be sheared in readiness for the height of summer. When the wool was sold it would earn their master a pretty profit. Hobart Hurst had many connections back in Derbyshire where the first mills had been opened. Folk of the moors had heard tell of these great factories that were opening, with mighty loom machines that weaved and prepared the cotton and wool. Machines, not hand woven. The output was said to be phenomenal. On the moors cloth and wool were still in the domain of cottage industries, people making for themselves what they needed. Some said the factory fabric would never take off, for who would buy machine made over the carefully tended home crafted? Others looked wary and shook their heads. Even if this was happening far away, it would be the beginning of the end. Life was going to change drastically.

The idea of machines taking over looked impossible on the clippings day. This work was done by hand, and by strong men. No machine could take over. The men were paid as daytal; in other words they were paid day by day. They were not on contract or yearly employment, and wouldn't have to wait till the end of the year to get their pay but the end of the day. Some were here because they hadn't been able to secure a hiring contract on one of the farms, others because they didn't like to be tied. Certainly those that had their own homes and families didn't want to be living away on a farm for a year as what felt like a lowly servant. They had grown into their independence. They would travel from farm to farm on the moors at this time of year, clipping the flocks of sheep. When they were done many would travel over to the dales, where everything happened a little later.

Amos Cornforth managed much of the running of the sheep farm on his own, but at shearing time, there was too much for one man. To get it done in a day they needed at least thirty men. Hobart Hurst had always been at the property for this day, with a hand on his purse and a careful eye on who was doing the work.

This year he was away in London and had entrusted the enterprise entirely to Amos. Although not on paper, Amos was back in his proper family place, master of the farm and managing the clippings.

Ellen Withers was in the kitchen swearing her Durham curses whilst trying to prepare enough cheesecakes, as they were called, to feed the hoards of men who would be shortly taking a break for ten o'clocks. Maud was stacking up plates with the flat, cheesy breads. Eleanor was busy with the fresh butter to smother on the cakes, wondering all the time what had happened to her diligent sister Gillian. Stephen sat on a cushion on a chair and delightedly ripped up a little cheesecake, given to him to keep him quiet. Somewhere outside Clara was working with Old Marsden on the finishing touches to a fresh salve to help aching joints.

Maud put some more cakes on the piled up plate, and a couple toppled off. Time to start a fresh pile. She wiped at her forehead with the back of her arm. It was a hot day and not the occasion to be at a blazing fire and busy with chores. "Eleanor, get these plates out onto the tables," she said, watching the eldest twin slide her forearms under two heavily laden metal platters to carry them outside. She shook her head to herself. "If I didn't know you two by the glance, I'd have thought you were Gillian."

Eleanor scowled. "I'm not lazy."

"No, but you've never been as domesticated as your sister. Have you seen her about?"

"No, she went off early. I don't know where."

"Not like our Gillian," Ellen said. "She's always been right reliable."

Always was meant to be broken, Eleanor supposed as she carried the platters of food outside. Gillian had been reliable, diligent and the worthy angel. But the last few weeks she'd been gone from the house a lot, and no one knew where she went. Not even Eleanor. Her sister had become a closed book. It had to be something serious, for Gillian never shirked her chores on busy days such as the clippings.

A few of the men were starting to gather for the first feed of the day. Three young men, including one of the Longbottoms, Frederick, who was now twenty-one, were loitering at the end of one of the tables, fingers hooked in waistcoat pockets and umming and ahing at one another as if they were great wise men. Their thoughts took a lower tone as Eleanor appeared, heaving plates of food onto the table. With the rushing around some of her hair had loosened from her hairpins, and framed her pink-cheeked face prettily. In the past year Eleanor Hurst had overtaken her sister quickly, and filled out into a woman. It had been noticed in the village, and commented upon many a time in the alehouse. Some felt she would be uncontrollable, expect too much from life. A young woman trotting all over the moors with her donkey, doing business? She wouldn't know her place in the kitchen. Some saw a positive angle only to their benefit in it. Some only thought of a bit of fun, so it did not particularly matter what the girl wanted for the rest of her life.

Eleanor was aware of the change in the way people, in particular the men looked at her. She didn't like it. Before, as a child she had been taken more seriously. Perhaps in mocking amusement, the little business lady with Assa transporting letters and goods about the land. Or playing her fiddle and pouring forth with strange tunes of goblins and Scots. But now all that was forgotten, a distraction of childhood. Now they would look at her form in a covetous way. Thinking about what they might do to her. She was just a body and a pair of hands to work in the kitchen now. She was under no illusion that she wouldn't escape the marriage fate for the rest of her life, but at the tender age of fourteen she was a long way from wanting to leave for the married home. And she was furious that her mind and her own self were being increasingly ignored.

Frederick Longbottom smiled at her. "You well, Miss Hurst?"

Before she had chance to reply one of his companions laughed and grabbed at her backside through her skirts. "This lass is more than well."

Before she realised what she was doing, she'd picked up the top cake, dripping in melted butter, and thrown it in the man's face. "Dirty pig!" she yelled at him. "You keep your swine trotters to yourself."

They ought to have been ashamed of themselves, but her outrage only seemed to encourage them more. She marched back to the kitchen, her hands balled up in taught fists by her sides.

The food and drink was soon delivered to the tables, and the daytal men crowded around, lined up on benches and cheerily started in on the food. Soon it would be consumed, they'd be back to work and the women would continue. Clear up the carnage and start work on the dinner. The roast was already on a spit cooking, for it took so many hours, but there were the puddings to boil and the rum sauce to prepare.

Eleanor was perched on a barrel to the edge of the scene, keeping out of the way. Ellen had said she ought to play the fiddle, get a bit of music going, but Eleanor was sulking after some of the comments she'd heard, and preferred to avoid further attention. She watched as a small, thin figure, with the pious movement of a nun, came walking steadily up the hill. Gillian.

Eleanor watched her sister with suspicion. It didn't look as though Gillian had noticed her, for she went to walk straight past Eleanor, probably distracted by the sheer number of people present for the clippings.

"Where have you been?"

Gillian jumped, looked around, then saw her sister. She wandered over. She looked bright and alive, far better than she had done the past couple of years. Her eyes were positively sparkling. Eleanor had noticed that things had been improving these weeks past, the moods and tantrums had stopped. Gillian was away out of the house a lot, although she didn't know where.

"You look happy," she added, as if she begrudged her sister peace of mind. "What's going on?"

Gillian couldn't keep the grin off her face. She stood beside Eleanor's barrel, but could barely keep still. "You mustn't say anything."

"What do you mean?"

"You must promise not to tell a soul."

Eleanor felt an unpleasant sense of apprehension creep upon her. "What have you done?"

Gillian clutched at her sister's hands. "Promise it. Oh, I'm so happy I have to tell someone, but it must be a secret."

"You're making me worried."

"Promise it. Promise you won't tell a soul."

"All right," Eleanor forced the agreement from her lips. "I won't tell anyone."

Gillian's grin broke even wider. "I'm getting married."

"Married?" Eleanor repeated dumbly. She hadn't even known that Gillian had a sweetheart. Oh certainly there was the one sided crush on William Longbottom, but that wasn't anything viable. Had someone come along and taken advantage of her misery. "What do you mean married? Do you mean betrothed?"

"No, I mean married." Gillian's bony fingers dug excitedly into Eleanor's hands, making her wince. "Before this year is out I'll be a married woman."

"But you're only fourteen!" Eleanor shrieked.

"Keep it down," Gillian hissed. "Fourteen's old enough. We're women now. Both you and I have started our bleeding..."

"Fourteen's too young." Eleanor looked away. She felt a little nauseous. They were too young to be rushing off to adulthood. Once a woman got married, that was it. Slavery and boredom, she didn't care about what all the folk songs and stories said about marriage being a girl's greatest joy.

"It's different for everyone," Gillian said, mildly patronising. "When you meet the right man, you'll see how you're suddenly ready."

Eleanor glowered into the middle distance. "You can't," she said with a sudden realisation. She was no expert on legal matters but she had listened in on conversations between her father and the local magistrate on many occasions. One evening the magistrate had been a little drunk, and laughing about old tales of secret marriages and the troubles they'd caused. The law men had reckoned that the new marriage act, brought in twenty odd years ago, would solve all that trouble. "You have to have mama and father's permission for the licence if you're under twenty one."

"We had the banns read for the first time at church this Sunday past," Gillian whispered in excitement.

"But mama or father could object. They'll hear about it soon enough. People will talk."

Gillian rolled her eyes. "We didn't go to Danby to get the banns read, silly. We're not daft. We're going to a different parish for the time being. No one knows."

Eleanor felt ill. With their father always away and their mother not always even managing to get to church at Danby, it was highly likely that Gillian would get away with this. And once she was married it would be too late. "Don't you think it's silly rushing into this marriage? You've been so crazed about William Longbottom for so long, and now to pick up with some other lad and just marry him on a whim. You'll regret this for the rest of your life."

"No I won't."

"Who is he anyway? Do I know him?"

"Of course you do." Gillian was near shaking with excitement. "It's William."

"William? William Longbottom? But he's in love with Megan Hammond."

"She broke the engagement off last year, as you well know." Gillian told her. "She can't have children, and she accepted that such a state is no good for a marriage."

"Just because she broke the engagement doesn't mean he stopped loving her."

"William wants a big family. I'm going to give him sons. Lots of sons."

She could see that her sister was completely blinded by her long term obsession with William. "Do you think it could be an idea to wait a bit?" she suggested tentatively. "Maybe leave it as an engagement for a couple of years. At least till you're sixteen. Then you could be sure of his affection..."

"Oh no, William's wanting to get started on the children as soon as possible. He's twenty four already. And I don't need to wait, I know what I want."

"But Gillian, this is a terrible mistake. William still loves Megan. He's just blinded because of her accident. You deserve more than this."

"He does love me," Gillian pulled angrily away. "He asked me. We're going to be married and we're going to be happy. You're just jealous."

"I am not. I'm only fourteen; I have no desire to be married."

"No one will have you. A wild girl who doesn't know a woman's place. No one's going to want you." Gillian hissed. "And if you tell anyone about this, I'll hate you forever." She ran off into the farmhouse before Eleanor had chance to come back with any smart retort. Stunned, Eleanor remained on her barrel seat and stared dumbly out to the fields. Her little world had abruptly been shook up and down. She was certain this decision would destroy her sister's life, but she was helpless. Gillian's mind wouldn't be changed, and Eleanor knew that she would keep her promise, no matter what. She would tell no one.

"I can't understand why anyone would want to get married," Eleanor exclaimed in a high flush of irritation. "After all of this, I don't think I shall ever get married."

The promise to tell no one was kept, and yet it was broken when she found herself confiding in her closest friends. Gillian would never know. As far as the family and the villagers went, Eleanor had said nothing. Even to the farmers' wives and inhabitants of neighbouring villages she could not say a word, because nothing travelled as fast as gossip across the moorlands. But she had told Atheleys that very same day when the two girls had met on the moors late that evening when the clippings were over. And it seemed that the frustration of the situation and the fact that she could talk to no one over it had brewed up to bursting point. The need to rant continued. To trusted non locals, she could not bite her tongue.

Her loud exclamation brought forth a little bray from Assa, and a cringing shuffle out of the Scot as they walked up the track towards Chequers Inn. Eleanor had spent the night at the inn, then followed the drovers' route south across the edge of the moors in the direction of Oldstead. She sometimes did this route and return in a day, making deliveries at the farms along the way. She hadn't made it as far as Oldstead this day, but had been pleasantly surprised to bump into Angus MacCaskill and wee Jamie the collie dog on their way back north. They'd back tracked a little with her to her final delivery at a farm, before all four, girl, man, dog and donkey, started on the four hour walk up to Chequers Inn.

Angus had cut his work in the south short as there was business he needed to get back to Scotland for. He had decided to return by foot to save on his earnings. Besides, he admitted, he was often jealous of the dogs getting to do the droving routes without the responsibilities of the cattle on the return journey. Last year's jaunt had been so pleasant he thought he might do it again. The wanderlust pulsed strong in his veins. This way he would get to see his favourite places and people for a second time in the year.

"So what you're saying is that you're a droving man in your blood."

"Aye, well," Angus shrugged it off, feeling a little self conscious although he couldn't quite bring himself to voice the issue on his mind. "Not yet. I've not got my licence, so all I do is assist my uncle."

"Why don't you just apply?"

He smiled. "It's not as simple as that. A man has to meet a certain number of criteria."

"You're not good enough?" Eleanor sounded surprised.

"For starters I'm not old enough."

Her eyebrows shot up. "But you must be dreadfully old."

He laughed out loud and heartily at her childish comment. For a child any adult seemed old. "I'm only twenty-six. I have to be thirty before I can apply for my licence."

"Four more years," Eleanor muttered. "Just think, in four more years you'll have your licence and I will be eighteen. Perhaps then I will feel like an adult."

"Well, you're only a lass the now."

"Maybe, but my sister doesn't seem to think so. She's getting married." And with that slip of the tongue, of a secret she wasn't meant to share, the whole sorry story came out for the second time.

Eleanor had tried to talk reason with her sister over the past weeks, but to no avail. She could not get Gillian to even admit to her when or where she and William would be married, so it would seem that there were to be no well wishers at the ceremony. Gillian had become a closed book. It seemed that she had grown far closer to their younger sister, Clara, who was often hanging around Gillian with a smug little smile on her china doll rosebud lips, whispering to her and tugging at her skirts. On one early Sunday morning, before the household was up and Gillian was sneaking out to start the long walk to her secret parish, Eleanor was already up and ready with the intention of following her sister to learn the truth. She was swiftly waylaid by little Clara, who unsettlingly seemed to know what Eleanor was about, and somehow in league with Gillian, was intent on keeping Eleanor outside of proceedings. She finished it with threats and insults, declaring that she knew how Eleanor was so jealous of her twin sister. Clara knew things. Clara could see things. She knew Gillian would have a long marriage. And she knew that Eleanor was jealous, because Eleanor would never be married properly in a church. It was short and hurtful, and long enough to allow Gillian to get away out of sight.

Eleanor had it out with her sister a few days later when Clara was away at Old Marsden's cottage. Although Gillian remained silent on the details of her impending marriage, her fury blurred her judgement and she did let some things slip. Although Eleanor could not work out the logic behind the guilt, it became clear that Gillian blamed herself for Megan Hammond's dreadful accident. It was a fact that William had his heart set on a large family. He had secured premises in the valley bottom of Commondale, close by the beck, for his smithy, and a family home around the back. He just needed a wife to keep house and procreate. Megan was no longer capable of that role, and it was all Gillian's fault. She was adamant that William would not suffer for it, and was stepping into the breach. William loved her for what she was offering to do for him. It was the stupidest reason for marriage Eleanor had ever heard, and she told Gillian so. Gillian gazed with pity upon her and declared her a child, with no appreciation of how the world really worked.

And so Gillian was married. Unknowingly, it was the decisive moment when so many other lives would be changed for better or worse, with consequences reaching much further than Gillian Longbottom, nee Hurst's marital home.

The morning when their routine idyll started to fall apart began as uneventfully as many mornings did. In the kitchen of Pines Lodge Maud sat with her eldest daughter, Eleanor, dictating a letter to a cousin over Haworth way with whom she had reconnected over the last few years. Although Maud had learnt the basics of letters, she did not read very well and her writing was slow and messy. Hardly fitting for the status she was supposed to hold, so she had one of the twins do her writing for her. Gillian wasn't to be found, and Eleanor had no plans to travel the moors today. She had even volunteered to do the writing. Clara was away at Old Marsden's and Ellen Withers was kneading bread at the other end of the kitchen table whilst pulling the occasional face at Stephen. He would whoop delightedly before returning to his play with the wild flowers Eleanor had picked from one of the lower meadows that morning.

The kitchen door opened without a knock and Gillian appeared on the threshold. She was flushed, looking full of excitement and terror simultaneously. Eleanor slowly lowered her pen onto the writing desk and felt a ball of nausea begin to revolve in her stomach. So it was done. Her eyes glanced down to her sister's hands, and as she knew what she was looking for, she quickly spotted the plain narrow ring.

"Gillian," Maud greeted her. "What did you do with yourself this morning? You must have been away at the crack of dawn."

"You weren't even about when I was up," Ellen Withers added as if to confirm just how early she must have left. She gave the dough another thump and rolled it up over itself.

"Mother, I have news," Gillian said breathlessly.

Eleanor closed her eyes. She could feel her sister's nerves, the way her heart was hammering in her chest.

"Oh?"

Ellen stopped kneading the bread and straightened. She'd been with the family so long there was no thought that she might need to leave the room.

Gillian took a breath, straightened herself as if to add more gravity to her announcement. I am not a small girl, but a grown woman. "I am married this morn."

What ever she had been expecting for a reaction, the dumb silence she received was not it. Maud and Ellen merely stared at her as if they were not quite sure what had been said. Eleanor was staring furiously at the half written letter and refusing to look at Gillian. The fire continued to crackle in its place. Moments felt like hours. Stephen was the first to break the deadlock, laughing and pulling petals from his flowers to throw at Gillian.

Ellen seemed to relax back into herself again as she laughed. "Oh, what silliness, girl," she said. "You haven't even got a sweetheart. What's happened, have you married yourself to our Lord?"

Gillian's face darkened.

Maud felt the old wound in the front of her jaw start to ache. She could tell that this was not a joke. "But you can't be," she said, "You're too young."

"Mother, it is done."

"But you would need permission. I never gave it, and I'm quite sure your father would never have agreed to it."

"We had the banns read in a different parish. It's all been done proper. I am a married woman."

"Oh god, Gillian," Maud gasped, putting her hand up to her mouth. She could feel her eyes filling with tears. That her daughter would have kept such secrets from her. "What have you done? You're only fourteen."

Gillian remained in the doorway, seemingly shrinking in size towards the uncertain girl.

Ellen pursed her lips. "You're in the family way. That's why you did it."

Maud squeezed her eyes shut. She had wanted more for her girls than the hasty marriage of necessity she had taken for herself. Even in her case she had been eighteen when she had been wed. A woman at least.

"I am still a virgin," Gillian hissed at Ellen. "I have my morals."

"But why would you do this if you didn't have to?" Maud cried. "You're only fourteen. You're still my little girl."

"Mama," Gillian felt her voice breaking. "I thought you would be happy for me."

"So which blackguard is it who's persuaded you to do such a thing?" Ellen asked. Her arms were folded across her chest, flour dust gently sprinkling to the floor.

"William Longbottom."

The gruff voice spoke from just behind Gillian. It sent an ice chill down the back of her neck, and a horror to her nerves. She had not thought he was at home. Unfortunately she had selected an inopportune day to be wed, when Hobart Hurst was also returning to his property in Commondale. He had arrived early and stopped off at the pub in the centre of the village for a drink and an early lunch before continuing to his home. It was there that he had overheard gossip and amusement directed at him, the foolish men not realising that the very target of their jesting was sat not more than three metres from them. They were laughing about the Hurst family, and what a merry jumble they were living in what had been home to the Cornforths' for so many generations. And would continue to be so for a good long time, if not in name then certainly in blood. Now that there was a male heir, dear little Stephen. Poor lad would be confused. With those fine curls and sweet face, any fool could see he had no connection to such a creature as Hobart Hurst. Still, it was all kept within the family, Hurst or Cornforth. They were quiet surprised Amos Cornforth had it in him to sire a son in such circumstances, given what a pathetic man he was. He should have taken his father in hand long before all the family money was gone. And then to stay on and work for the man who had now taken over all his family's inheritance. What a weakling of a man. Still, it looked as though he'd had his revenge.

Gillian could sense the anger emanating from her father. She did not realise that much was focused in his gaze upon the little boy. He had silently left the pub, only to bump into Mary Longbottom who had excitedly told him about William and

Gillian's union. Another local man to make a mockery of him, it would seem. One man to take his wife and sire a son. Another to take a daughter without so much the common decency to ask for Hobart's permission. Of course he would never have given it, for he had plans of an alliance through Gillian's marriage which would never happen now.

"It seems I have been absent from this farm too long," Hobart said evenly. "For none of you can be trusted to manage your lives decently."

Everyone apart from Stephen, who was too young to know better, shrank in horror. They could feel the menace in Hobart's voice. The lack of movement was unsettling. They had seen his anger and his violence before. His displeasure was never shy in making itself known. Nothing had been quite as shocking as Gillian's marriage. The very fact that he wasn't hitting people with his stick, roaring and red faced, terrified them even more.

Gillian foolishly broke the eye of the storm. "I am an honest and decent married woman."

"You are a deceitful little whore!" Hobart boomed in her ear. "With no respect for your father. Why else would you go sneaking to get married in clandestine circumstance?" He grabbed a fistful of her dress at the shoulder and dragged her up to his eye. "And now, Mrs Longbottom," he sneered in her ear with hot breath. "Get back to your own house, for you do not live here."

"But I wanted to collect my things."

"Your things?" he shouted. Gillian squeezed her eyes shut, tears racing down her face. Her whole body trembled. "There is nothing in this house for you."

"But father..."

"I'm not your father. You are not of my blood. I owe you nothing." He swung her bodily around and out of the house into the yard.

Eleanor was numb. She felt herself trying to ask what did he mean. There was no sound from her voice. But if Gillian was not of his blood, then neither was she. The question had to be where did she come from? As much as she disliked her father, she had always known him to be her kin. Her parent.

Gillian let out a scream as she tumbled onto the rough ground, scrapping her knees. Maud jolted up from the table. "Husband!" she called, hurrying out of the farmhouse. Ellen and Eleanor went to the window, either too fearful or too shocked to go out into the fray.

Outside Hobart kicked Gillian in the rump and sent her sprawling, spread eagled in the dirt. "What happened, you ungrateful wench? Have you got a bastard in your belly? Just like your mother are you?"

Maud pulled at his arm. "Please, she's just a girl."

"She's a married woman." He threw his wife off. "And she can get off my property. I will kick you all the way to William Longbottom, do you hear me?"

Gillian staggered up, sobbing violently. She started to totter away from the building. Hobart swiped at her with his walking stick. "Off my property, and don't you dare come back."

Maud was distraught. "Husband, please..."

Ellen and Eleanor watched as Hobart ignored his wife and marched to the moors. Gillian stumbled away down the track into the village. Maud remained like a shadow as her little home crumbled about her. Eleanor clutched to the window frame as she watched the drama. "What did he mean?" she asked quietly, looking to Ellen. "He was just angry, when he said Gillian's not his daughter?"

Ellen wrung her hands in her apron. She shook her head. "You have his name but that's all. Not a drop of blood you share with that beast, and you be thankful for it. The less of his kin that's on the earth, the better. It's just a miracle that Miss Clara turned out as sweet as she did."

Except that she's not sweet, Eleanor thought to herself. I fear she's quite deadly.

As the days rolled by, the Hurst family slipped into a feeling of comfort, assuming that Hobart would be gone for months as he always was. Perhaps even longer, to wait for his fury over Gillian's secret marriage to cool. Life returned to normal to a certain extent, although Gillian was now absent from their home, and did not dare show her face at Pines Lodge.

Ann Longbottom, mother to William, came up to the property that first evening. The news had swept through the village with the ferocity of a wild fire, as all good gossip goes. Her eldest, William, had come to her that morning to announce that he was wed, to little Gillian Hurst from up the hill. She still couldn't get over the hurt that this had been kept such a secret from her. Her own child wed, and she had known nothing about it. William had protested that they had nothing to be ashamed of, although the very fact that it had all been done in such secret left her uncomfortable.

She found Maud Hurst hunched up on a little barrel outside the farmhouse. She was alone, Ellen having taken little Stephen and Clara in hand, and Eleanor having wandered out onto the moors to discuss the day's events with her friend. Maud was in stunned shock. How could her own daughter have neglected to share such an event with her? And how could any mother not know? Deeper down there was an unsettled worry that she now had a married child. Soon she could be a grandmother. She did not feel old enough for such status. She was only thirty-two and yet it felt as though her best years were behind her. What did she have to show for it? A clean and ordered home, wild girls who did what they pleased and had no thought to the consequences nor anyone else, and a husband who was hardly ever here. For all she knew, he could have two or three more such households across the country.

Ann looked at her neighbour with concern. She was now in her forties, but looked older, worn out from hard work and lengthy childbearing that was still potentially not over, although thankfully she had lost the most recent early on. "Maud," she spoke, catching the thoughtful woman's attention. "I've come to speak, parent to parent."

Maud thumbed at her skirts. "Mr Hurst is not at home."

"I heard he went off in a temper."

"He is rarely at home."

"It does not matter, for my husband has not come. He is too angry himself."

"I don't suppose he wanted Gillian as a daughter in law."

"Oh my dear, it's nothing like that," Ann hurried up to her. Maud shuffled to give her a little space on the barrel top to sit. "It is the secrecy of it all. They say they have only done right, but they know we would never have allowed it had they asked. Your Gillian is too young."

"She is, indeed she is. I have felt I have lost her for months past. I had no idea she was planning this."

"You should not blame yourself."

"I am sorry for her. I know William was sweet on Megan Hammond. I suppose he did not want her for a wife, as she could not have a child."

"I know, but I had hoped they would remain together," Ann admitted. "Imagine what a life they might have had, Maud.

Imagine the running of a house but without the work and pain of so many children. Can you imagine what Megan's life might have been like, why, she might have been able to do something, a job like a man."

Both women tittered at this suggestion, wiping at sad eyes and sighing that they should laugh on such a day.

"There is a lot to be said for marrying someone you love. I know your Gillian stares at my William like a lovesick pup, but it is not the same. As for William, I cannot say what he was thinking."

"It is done now."

"Aye," Ann nodded. "It is done before God, and it cannot be undone. They will both have to live with the consequences of this decision. I hope it works for them." She looked over at Maud. "Give it some days for the dust to settle. Things will be all right, and Mr Hurst will calm down. We still have our other children to take solace in."

Unfortunately things did not transpire in that fashion.

A week later, on a pleasant morning, when the weather suggested nothing terrible could happen, everything changed. Ellen Withers was in the kitchen with Clara and Stephen playing with some cut flowers on the table. Clara was trying to teach her young brother to weave a blossom ring, rather unsuccessfully. Eleanor was preparing her saddlebag for her journey over to Chequers, with letters and goods to be delivered. Maud was outside in the yard talking to Amos Cornforth. Gillian had not returned home to see her kin, and although the family knew the little cottage by the river where William and Gillian now resided, no one dared to pay a visit. Each side was fearful of the fury from the other.

From further up the track a cart pulled by an old nag rattled down towards the farm. Along with the driver sat a grim faced Hobart Hurst, and a dark and swarthy unknown man with a stern stare, and a general ambience of cruelty. The cart stopped outside the farm, Hobart waving a distracted hand at the driver and giving some instruction. Whilst the cart was turned around to return the way it had come, Hobart and the stranger marched into the yard with a distinct sense of propriety.

The conversation between Maud and Amos faltered as they looked in confusion at the arrival. Maud stepped forward, moving to greet her husband for the sake of etiquette, but he held up a hand to silence her.

"Mr Cornforth, this is for you," he explained, handing Amos a small purse.

With the naivety of the trusting, he accepted the purse. "What's this for?"

"Your wages to see the month out."

"But I..."

Maud felt nauseous. She had been foolish to think that Hobart would not set things back to his rule.

"Might I introduce Mr Hodgkin," he said, gesturing to the unsmiling man beside him. "He is my new farm manager with immediate effect. We will no longer require your services, Mr Cornforth, and I would be grateful if you quit my premises immediately so that no case of trespass need be brought."

"But Mr Hobart, I've worked this farm well..." Amos began to protest.

"Husband, we have no need to doubt Mr Cornforth's work. He's done well by us," Maud began, feeling a desperation clutch at her chest. She couldn't live here without seeing him every day. She lived on those kind words and sweet glances.

"I think Mr Cornforth's breeding projects have gone far beyond the requirements of his post," Hobart hissed at her. "And you," he added, raising his walking stick and looking back to Amos. "I believe I asked you to quit my property. You have your pay, now kindly depart."

Amos looked sadly from Hobart to Maud. This was the penalty when one had their way with another man's wife. But little Stephen was a joy, and now he would not be able to see him. He would not be able to talk with Maud each morning, to stroll with her about the property and imagine in some foolish way that this was still his home. This was his punishment for he had been immoral.

"Oh no," Maud wailed.

"Mr Hodgkin," Hobart began his instruction as he pushed his wife away from Amos Cornforth. "Please make sure Mr Cornforth does not set foot on my property again. He is not needed here by any of us."

Bewildered and heartbroken, Amos started to walk away. Mr Hodgkin snapped at his heels, telling him to 'git'.

"Ellen Withers," Hobart roared whilst clutching on to the collar of his wife's dress to stop her running after their corrupting farm manager. He was immune to her sobs. He looked to the house, and saw Ellen and Eleanor watching from the window, both with pale and frightened countenances. Ellen jumped when he looked to the window, and disappeared from view only to reappear in the doorway.

"Yes, sir?"

"Go inside and pack Miss Clara's trunk. I want it ready in ten minutes."

Ellen faltered. "Sir?"

"Go and pack Clara's things. Now."

Ellen looked from husband to wife, before a flash from Hobart's eyes sent her shuffling back inside.

"What are you doing with my Clara?"

"You are clearly incapable of raising girls to become ladies, which should not have been a surprise to me given what a loose whore you are. Clara shall go to stay with a good family of breeding and reputation in Thirsk."

"Thirsk? But that's such a league away. Please don't take my children from me."

Inside the kitchen, now with all the doors open, the children could hear every word that was being spoken out in the yard. Clara clapped her dainty china hands together. "I am going to live in Thirsk," she said. "I believe that's further than even you have been, Eleanor."

Eleanor glared at her.

"I shall become a real lady and lord it over all of you."

Stephen laughed, not understanding what was happening.

It would be an adventure to travel to Thirsk, Eleanor thought a little enviously. But she did not want to go anywhere her father might send her. And to go to Thirsk to live, why that would have meant she would not see her friends, go on her long walks with Assa, or see the drovers again. Thank goodness he didn't want to send her away to be a lady.

"Eleanor Hurst, get out here!"

Eleanor darted back from the window and looked back into the kitchen. Clara grinned at her, like a cat toying with its prey. "I wonder what he's going to do with you."

"I'm staying here."

Clara snorted. "You're not."

Eleanor stepped to the doorway, staring at the wretched scene before her. Hobart Hurst stood in barely controlled fury, the vein down his forehead throbbing. Maud was sagging on her feet, supported only by his grip on her dress. She sobbed deeply and achingly, as if for the end of the world.

"I'm staying here," Eleanor repeated.

"You are not," Hobart retorted. "This thing isn't fit to raise girls." He shook her mother at her. "You want to be a little business lady. Well, we shall train you properly so you can be of use to your future husband. Go and pack and a bag, for you and I are walking to Whitby today."

"Whitby? I'm not going to Whitby."

"You will, and you will live there and do as you are told. Now get inside and pack what you can carry."

Eleanor hesitated, hoping for a moment that her mother would do something to save her from this fate. Mr Hodgkin stood like a sentry in the yard, his thumbs tucked into his belt and his chest puffing out his waistcoat. This was hopeless; she had no say in any of this.

She stepped back into the house just as Ellen was hobbling out with Clara's trunk.

"Get that into the cart," Hobart instructed. "And get Clara ready for riding, she's to travel to Thirsk immediately."

Clara laughed as Eleanor reappeared. "You must walk, but I shall ride in a carriage."

"It's a dirty old farm cart and it's more than you deserve, you little witch."

Clara bared her teeth.

In her room, Eleanor hurriedly emptied the saddle bags out onto the bed. Her hands were shaking. What had Gillian done to them all by getting married? She knew this was not Gillian's intention, but she was furious with her twin and for a moment felt that she could hate her. What to take? She gathered up her letters, her books and music sheets and carefully packed them. Her fiddle was in its case, and took the remaining space in the final saddle bag. Her few clothes and hairbrush filled the other bag. That was it. So easy to leave. She stood back from the bed and felt tears prick her eyes.

Ellen quietly came into the room. "Miss Clara has departed."

Eleanor didn't care.

"Your father wants to set off now."

"I don't want to go. Can't Mama say anything?"

"You know we're all at his mercy."

"I haven't said goodbye to anyone."

"I know, but you have to hurry before he gets too angry. He'll start hitting." Ellen clutched at her shoulders.

"I'll take Assa..."

"He said the donkey has to stay here."

"Am I to have no friend with me?" Eleanor wailed.

"I'm sorry my sweet girl," Ellen was almost whispering, her voice shaking. "I'll take good care of her." She looked to the jumble on the bed. "Are these all the things you were meant to deliver?"

"I was supposed to go to Chequers today."

"Don't worry, I'll sort all this."

"I don't want to go."

"I know." Ellen hugged her close. "You take good care of yourself, and get back as soon as he'll let you."

"I shall never be home," Eleanor moaned. "He'll have me married off to some drunkard fisherman."

"I doubt it. He uses us as pawns, and you'd be better played making connections with rich merchants." Ellen kissed the top of her head. "Away with you before we have any more trouble."

She slung one of the bags over her shoulder, the other was to carry. Like a woman to the execution block, Eleanor left the house, remembering to scoop up her shawl and hat on the way out. Her mother hijacked her as she left the threshold, hugging her tightly and kissing her hair. "Take care and you write me. Come home soon. I will miss you."

"Get off her woman, we have a long walk ahead of us."

Eleanor hugged her mother back. "Goodbye mother," she whispered. "Until I next see you again."

Although it would have been quicker to Whitby walking across the moorlands following the way marker stones, Hobart Hurst had decided they would instead follow the river. They trekked down the Esk Valley as it wound its way down to the coast and Whitby. She assumed it was a choice of whim and gave it no more thought. What Eleanor did not know was that Atheleys was loitering on the moors above Commondale with a rock in her hand, watching the paths and those who decided to stride out onto the hills.

It was easier walking following the river in the valley, but it also meant passing through the little villages of the Esk. Eleanor felt questioning eyes upon her. The first stretch was familiar, walking through places she knew, and where the people knew her. From Commondale they walked to Castleton, and onwards to Danby. She could sense that people wanted to ask where she was going, and without Assa at that, but Hobart Hurst's overwhelming countenance held back any approach.

From Danby they walked through open country, passing by farms but seeing few people, and skirting around the hamlet of Howlsyke completely. They walked through Lealholm and were on the approach to Glaisdale when Eleanor was flagging and wished to stop. Hobart refused and instead demanded that they pick up the pace. At first she thought he was doing this purely to torture her, for all female Hursts deserved punishment in his eyes. But as the silent march continued she noticed that her father appeared to actually be nervous. His eyes would flit from copse of trees to hawthorn scrub, as if expecting someone to be waiting there. He muttered something about wanting to be quickly out of the range of Hart Hall before they might rest. The sight of some rags from a torn shirt caught on a thorn bush sent him in a near panic, and he almost broke into a jog. There was an oddly aggressive feel to the air, as if they were trespassing and not welcome in this district.

Hobart Hurst tripped on a tree root and for a moment hovered between balance and sprawling into the mud. He skipped forward to beat the fall, and managed to stay on his feet. Halting, he shook himself and seemed to calm, muttering that of course 'he' would be out flailing now, and would not have the time to bother them. But they did not stop until they reached the little village of Egton Bridge, nestled down in the depths of a steep sided wooded valley.

They stopped at an old inn near the river, by the name of the Horseshoe Inn, and took an early supper before embarking on the last few hours to get to Whitby. Eleanor had never been this far down the valley, and although she loved to explore, she did not wish to be in his company. She wished she could run away, but where would she go, other than home? He would return, and perhaps even beat Mama because her child was such an unruly girl. She looked across the inn table at her father and thought him ugly and old. He did not fit with their family. She thought of her mother, crumpled in the yard sobbing, and felt her throat tighten. He was a wicked man.

"You should not have called Mama a whore."

Hobart ceased shovelling the stew into his mouth and gazed across at Eleanor, surprised that she had been so bold as to say such a thing to him. "I speak the truth."

"It is a lie. Such women take pennies from men, and she has never taken any money. Except from you."

His fingers coiled tightly around the spoon and threatened to crush it. "You ought to watch your mouth, girl. It is too smart for a woman. You mind your manners or you'll find yourself in trouble. You know they're taking women into the gaols at York now?"

He was an idiot. "I've done nothing wrong."

"And when did that ever stop punishment?"

"I..." He had caught her with that thought. "You are saying Mama is innocent?"

He ignored her question and instead leaned over the table like a little ogre. "There was a man born in this village, you know. Went by the name of Postgate. He was a very good man, followed the religious path and went into the church. Now wouldn't you say there's a man who's done nothing wrong?"

Eleanor hunched into herself. "I suppose," she muttered, although she was not convinced membership in a church automatically confirmed one's goodness for eternity.

"He ended up in York prison. They executed him in a most terrible way. Hung, but still alive, and then drawn and quartered. Sliced up like a pig, whilst still alive. He would have seen his own innards before his dying eyes..."

Eleanor closed her eyes.

Hobart cleared his throat. "Just you mind you don't end up in there."

"Why did they kill him?"

"Followed the God in the wrong way. He was a Catholic."

She opened her eyes and watched Hurst as he cleared his bowl. Why did he always speak of things, society and religion and communities as if it were nothing to do with him?

"Get your food finished." He broke the thoughtful mood. "We've got a good few hours walking ahead of us. We'll not stop till we get to Whitby."

It was growing dark when they arrived at the coastal port of Whitby. A thick sea fret was rolling off the North Sea and up the mouth of the River Esk. Most of the steep town was lost from view, with only the eerie sounds of bells, workers' shouts and the clatter of donkeys' feet (but not Assa, Eleanor thought regretfully) pattering through narrow winding streets little more than passageways through the mesh of buildings. Hanging lanterns and lights from windows pushed out an eerie glow, fighting against the encroaching mist. It felt cold and dank, and the air was filled with a salty, fishy smell Eleanor was not used to. She shrank back into the bunched shawls she kept around her body and followed Hobart Hurst through the labyrinth of streets. Soon she was very lost, in what felt like a sprawling metropolis. She would never find her way out again. A lost soul. How would she ever survive here?

Hobart owned a property in town. It was a three story house crammed in at awkward angles against a sloping street. The ground floor was for his business, with the kitchen out the back, where there was also a yard, an alcove where the maid slept, and an outdoor privy. The first floor held a dining room for entertaining important clients, and Hurst's own rooms. Up in the attic there was storage and also a slanting cold room that was to be Eleanor's quarters. There was no curtain on the small window, and the room was sparsely furnished, with a shabby little bed, wooden chair and table with a chipped washstand. A blackened fireplace that did not appear as though it had been used in years and no bookshelves. Eleanor stood in the threshold and felt her heart break. Her father informed her she might fit it out as she saw fit tomorrow, and left her for the night, closing the door firmly behind him.

She dropped her bags to the ground and walked across to the bed. Sitting down, she was aware that there were other inhabitants in the bed, bugs and the like. She sprang up with a look of disgust on her face. Did folk live like pigs here? Mama and Ellen Withers had always kept the home clean and pleasant. Apparently there was a full time maid here, but she couldn't see that anything had been done. It was a shabby and infested hole. This was to be her refuge from whatever Hurst had planned. This was nothing short of a punishment, and she had done nothing wrong. It was her sister who had gotten married in secret. She had not even told her own twin, her own half of the marriage date. She got to run off and live with her idol whilst the rest of them were punished. Even Clara had been sent away, although Eleanor suspected her younger sister would find herself in far better circumstances and enjoying a certain level of luxury.

She sat down on the chair and propped her feet up on the cold fire grate. This was disgusting. There clearly was little respect for her if this was to be her lodging, but tomorrow she would start and change things. She would make the best of this as she could until she was able to get away and back to the moors.

Eleanor slept fitfully in her propped position in the chair. As light came in through the window in the morning she was up, ready to start the work. When she opened the door she found the maid, Lucy Ann, yawning on the steps. She was a young, thin thing with ragged dirty clothes and unkempt hair sticking out from under her mop cap. Given the way her father liked to have things at home, she was surprised he was happy to live this way in Whitby.

"Miss, do you want anything?"

Eleanor, grouchy from lack of sleep, threw her bags out onto the landing. "It is a disgrace in there, what kind of a maid are you?"

The girl's eyes widened. "But I was told..."

"I want a great many things," Eleanor wasn't interested in what the girl had to say today. She had consulted her book by Hannah Glasse before she'd dropped off to sleep. Although it was mostly a cook book, there was advice on keeping house, including a very helpful page on the fumigation of rooms. "I want rough blankets to cover the window, fireplace and doors in this room. I want a large broad pan and I want a bag of charcoal. A pound of rolled brimstone..."

Lucy Ann's lips were moving soundlessly as she wrote the list down in her memory. This had been quite a good job up until now, for she really only had to do anything when Mr Hurst was in residence, otherwise the clerk was in the office and he kept that clean himself. But Mr Hurst had told her Miss Hurst was to be obeyed without question or attitude, and whilst Lucy Ann would normally had been inclined to sullenness with someone as young, haughty and fine looking as Miss Hurst (it was all very well being judgemental when you hadn't been raised in poverty), she was too terrified of Mr Hurst to do anything but be obedient.

"And when you get back from fetching all of that, I want the biggest container on the boil that we have. We'll be washing all this bed linen." By nightfall tonight there would be no bugs living in her room. "Let's get to it; these are only the jobs for the morning." If she had not been so tired and grumpy, she would not have had such confidence with her authoritarian attitude.

Eleanor had the bed stripped. One piece was so tatty and louse-ridden that she slung it straight into the kitchen fire, listening to the bugs pop as they burned alive. In the attic the two girls covered over the window and fireplace with rough sheets, then filled the pan with charcoal and brimstone in the centre of the room. Lighting the mixture of shards, they hurried out, shutting the door and blocking up the gaps with another old sheet. That would be left for a good six hours before re-entry. The work to clean out the room would then begin, with a fully opened window.

With the upper floor out of bounds for six hours, they went down to the belly of the property to the kitchen. Eleanor and Lucy-Ann worked at the laundry of bed sheets, whilst also starting to get the kitchen in some order. Eleanor was truly surprised by the disorder of the domestics of the house. Lucy Ann told her that Mr Hurst had hired a cook who had looked after all the food and the dining room upstairs, but he had fired her but a week ago and left Lucy Ann, who didn't know a thing about cooking, in charge of everything. Neither the cook nor Lucy Ann understood what he was about, for Mr Hurst's whims were illogical and temperamental. The clerk, who looked after the books for Mr Hurst's trading business and dealt with clients and dealers when Mr Hurst was away, was on tenterhooks, and with good reason. At noon Hurst returned from business in town and fired his clerk as well. There had been shouting in the front office, then a slamming of doors. In the kitchen the girls, who had been eating their lunch, prepared by Eleanor, looked at one another.

"I can't believe you're his own daughter," Lucy Ann, who was still to learn the place of a servant, whispered to Eleanor. She'd initially thought the girl a stroppy, spoilt brat by the way she'd spoken first thing that morning. But Eleanor had gotten stuck in with the work alongside her, and Lucy Ann felt as though she'd actually learned a few pointers about running a house. Much of Lucy Ann's problem and root of timidity was that no one had really thought to explain to her the work and duties. She was only eleven and didn't know much about looking after a household. She was just used to doing what the cook had told her, and when Mr Hurst was away, the cook didn't set foot in the property either. On such occasions Lucy Ann was in the house on her own. The clerk had never wanted much to do with her, and so she'd sit in the alcove a lot, humming and playing with a couple of little ragdolls she had made. When her solitude grew too much and she was feeling bored, she would go out into one of the closes to play with the fishermen's children.

Hobart Hurst entered the kitchen, and both of the girls jumped up from the table as if standing to attention. Neither were bidden nor trained to react so, the atmosphere prompted them to their feet. There was a gravity about Eleanor's arrival that suggested everyone's fates had been decided today.

He looked from one to the other. "Lucy Ann, you are now the maid of all work."

Lucy Ann took on an ashen pallor. She didn't know how to cook. She didn't know the order of things for running a house. She was used to simple chores and doing as she was bidden.

"Miss Hurst will instruct you where your knowledge is lacking."

Eleanor's eyes widened. What was she supposed to know about running a house?

Hurst handed Eleanor an iron ring with a number of keys. "These are the keys to the house. You are now in charge of running this house and dealing with the staff..."

"But..."

He handed her a second, more civilised set of keys. "These are to the study, the safe and the business cupboards. You shall be taking over the clerk's duties."

"I don't know anything about being a clerk."

"I shall teach you what you need to know, starting tomorrow. Then you will be able to manage things here in my absence."

"And when will I be going home?"

He looked at her as if she was a fool. "This is your home." He regarded them both in silence, then parted with one final comment before heading out on business. "It's sink or swim time, girls."

The months flicked over in an ever increasing blur. Lucy Ann and Eleanor floundered and paddled in circles. Somehow they kept their heads above water and learned to swim. Parts of the household were neglected as they learned their arts. Time keeping and an ability to manage their chores was work in progress. Things became easier as Lucy Ann grew more confident and could be relied upon to get on with certain tasks without needing to be asked, and Eleanor found more time for her own work, and even some time to entertain herself. As she began to learn the community of Whitby, she realised that they were not quite the oddity she had first assumed – a household and business matters run by women. Whitby itself was an oddity for the time, with women having to take on financial matters and business dealings out of necessity to cover the long months when their men were away of the whaling ships that sailed out of the port.

With just two to run a business and a house, the first job to be outsourced was the washing. Laundry could take days, and with everything else to be done, there simply was not the time for it. Lucy Ann had been sent into service at an early age as the bulging family needed the money. Mrs Argument, the matriarch of a screaming, tumbling hoard of uncountable children, took in the washing and was glad of the work that Eleanor was able to send her way.

With Hannah Glasse's book at their side, Eleanor and Lucy Ann learned the art of the kitchen together. There was a certain amount Eleanor had picked up from home, but the variety of food available in Whitby was fresher and bountiful. These things had been easy enough when she was just helping Ellen Withers out when the mood took her. Here she was alone, and had a maid looking to her for guidance. It suddenly seemed like an overwhelming feat to manage. Fish became a staple every day. Some of the oddest creatures appeared with Mr Hurst. Once he dropped a heron unceremoniously on the table. Eleanor had seen the tall, leggy birds fishing in the streams around Commondale, but she had never known anyone eat a heron. They had looked at the gangly legged large bird, glassy eyed and still on the large kitchen table without a thought of what to do with it. Naturally Ms Glasse's book had all the instruction they needed.

Hurst's house cramped its way amongst other properties clustered on steep banks. Whitby was built on both sides of a river that cut jaggedly through crumbling coastal land and out to the sea. Above the outer reaches of the compact whaling port there were crumbling cliffs and a ruined abbey set high up above the town on windswept grasslands where locals managed their cattle. Salt, the stink of fish and songs of faraway lands blew in on sea winds up the little estuary to wind around in the tightly packed closes and narrow streets that were little better than corridors. Whitby was a busy place and people were busy at business, plying their trade and earning a living. Being by the sea, shipping formed the foundations of most enterprises, and through holding shares in many boats, Hurst had his fingers in most of the pies.

There were great shipbuilding yards that constructed boats for all enterprises, from local fishing to working for the big London-based companies and transportation and exploration across the globe. James Cook had been apprenticed at the Quaker Yard long before Eleanor had come to Whitby although the apprentice lads would still chatter about the man and his adventures whilst at work on their carpentry. At night they would dream about what might come of them in the future. Now Captain Cook, who had discovered Australia, was out sailing the Pacific Ocean, and places so foreign Eleanor could barely imagine it. She never got to lay eyes on the great man, although others said they had seen him, spoken to him, even worked with him. But he was killed whilst she was living Whitby under Hurst's rule, rumour had it eaten by cannibals. After that one or two of the apprentice shipwrights wondered if a quieter life on the Yorkshire coast might not be such a bad thing.

There was a toll drawbridge across the river connecting the two sides of the town. Many of the lower houses near the water had their own little boats, and to avoid paying a toll, in a reminiscent way of how the drovers would take the harder, steeper roads, to save their money from the toll roads, people would row back and forth taking themselves and goods to the other side. Hurst's house was no exception. From her attic window Eleanor would watch the business of the port, the world suddenly a much smaller place. This was the opposite of the great open expanses of the moorlands. Here the whole world muddled through on top of one another and the cliffs loomed up over the horizon so one could not see for miles across the land. Whitby-built ships now working for the Russia Company of London would arrive with loads of Russian timber for building. Wood grown in faraway places as Russia! Eleanor's mind danced with excitement. It was so big and busy here compared to her home of Commondale, and so incredibly cosmopolitan. This must be what London was like, she rather naively told herself.

Along with his shares in the cargo and fishing boats, Hobart Hurst also had shares in the heavy duty ships that went up to the ice waters of the north to hunt whales. The great beasts of mythical size were transported back to Whitby. The corpses were butchered up north on the sea out of necessity, and in Whitby the great hunks of body were chopped up further and the blubber sent off to blubberhouses deeper in the town. Hurst owned one such blubberhouse, where whale blubber was processed and turned into whale oil that was used all over the country for lamps and lubrication. The bones were highly prized in fashion for ladies stays and corsets. Hurst had contacts in all the big cities selling to the tailors and fashion houses that dressed the best of society. Eleanor was not to be excluded, and was provided with the best whalebone which seamstresses used to provide her with waist-pinching undergarments, over which pretty dresses could be hung.

She learnt the Whitby end of the business, how to keep the accounts and books and deal with contacts and traders in Hurst's absence. She kept up with correspondence with traders and contacts in other cities, and although this was only a corner of Hurst's business empire, she began to understand just how much money was flowing through his hands. Her mama could have been kept in a palatial townhouse with an army of servants to tend to her needs, and yet he kept her in a farmhouse, albeit a very comfortable property, and better than many of the other Commondale locals, but still a bargain in comparison to what his wealth could have afforded.

She also dealt with the wages, and the men and women who thought they could mislead a young woman into overpaying soon learned that although Eleanor was kind, she was nobody's fool. Not even her father's, for when it dawned on her she was not taking a clerk's wage, or any other type of wage, so thus not even earning the pittance that little Lucy Ann took home, she decided on a fair and generous wage, never once thinking that as a female clerk she ought to earn less than a male counterpart. Hurst was away at the time, so she wrote a letter to his London residence to let him know she had corrected this oversight. When an angry letter returned saying family members did not need a wage from the business, especially those who were fed and watered, dressed with fine clothes and sheltered by a roof over their head, she ignored him and threw the letter in the river. She would earn her living, and through that her independence, for she was determined to leave this place one day.

There was much to learn and experience, and Whitby became close to her heart, but she missed her friends and family desperately. Her father left her alone to manage the house and accounts. Her solitary responsibility meant travel away from Whitby was out of the question most of the time. It left Eleanor with only letters to keep in touch with her dearest. Not everyone knew how to write. Atheleys was out of the question, for even though Eleanor doubted she knew her letters, there was no place to direct anything to her childhood friend. It was with her mother that the letter writing fared best. Maud did not have the best handle on the pen, nor particularly good spelling, but Stephen was growing up into a grand little scholar who learned the art of writing very quickly. He took regular dictated letters from his mother, adding his own sections, and pieces of advice and recipes from Ellen who was most worried about such a house with only Eleanor and Lucy Ann, both inexperienced girls, to run it. Maud would add sections she could not bear to dictate to her son, in her rough childish hand.

It took some months and coaxing before Gillian was prepared to resume contact with her twin. It was a fact that infuriated Eleanor, for the other siblings were being punished for Gillian's indiscretions, and yet she gave them the cold shoulder as if they were at fault. Gradually their communications increased, although on certain matters Gillian would not speak, as it were, through the pen. For, as she informed Eleanor, as an unmarried maiden, she was not experienced or mature enough to understand some things. Eleanor, running a household, keeping accounts and dealing with traders, not all of them English, scoffed at Gillian's snotty and foolish attitude, but chose to ignore it, rather than trying to goad her sister into admitting the reality of their circumstances.

She exchanged short notes with Mrs Barker, who admitted herself she was not known for her craft of written conversation. Instead she sent jars of moorland honey, little pieces of embroidery one of her daughters had created for Eleanor, and springs of blooming heather. Eleanor sent back equally odd trinkets: little jars of whale oil, linens and a small jet pendant to Mrs Barker's daughter in thanks for the embroidery. She would also include lengthy letters that looked more like packages so thick they were, to be kept to one side for when the drovers came and might be passed to Angus MacCaskill. She missed being able to time her visits to Chequers with when the drovers were passing through. No longer could they stroll and talk for hours or that he might teach her a new jig on the fiddle. She wasn't sure if Angus would notice her absence on the moors, or even be interested in her long accounts of life in Whitby and all that had happened. Months went by, then in the late autumn a parcel came from Chequers along with the usual communication from the Barkers. There was a long letter from Angus, who as she gratefully realised, had a fine and literate hand. The letter told almost all that had happened to him, wee Jamie and the other drovers over the summer. He stayed up all night on arrival at Chequers on learning what had happened, writing out all he had to say to Miss Hurst. Or most of what he wanted to say at least. Between the pages there was a gift he said he had been carrying with him for months: a small silver thistle pendant. Eleanor was so thrilled she never took it off. Now that he knew where she was in Whitby, he was able to send letters from different parts of the country wherever the droving sent him, but Eleanor was stuck with communicating through Chequers. There was mention of coming through Whitby to see her, but it never happened, for the following years he was travelling more to the west side of the country, learning the droving routes down to Carlisle and into Cumbria and the Lakes, heading to places such as Manchester.

Eleanor was busy but as she learned her work she grew more efficient and had increasing time to herself. In evenings by lamp light she spent hours writing her letters. She took to exploring Whitby, walking along by the docksides and through the narrow streets, up to the markets on the far side of the river. One evening when the sea fog pulled in, she was startled as a great black, and seemingly rabid dog, leapt down from a ship and rushed past her, disappearing into the town with only the sound of its angry barks to signal it had ever been there. Press gang officers looking to bulk up the navy were about looking for young fisherman and apprentice shipwrights to take out of Whitby and onto the high seas.

Hobart Hurst left nothing to chance, although Eleanor was unaware of his greater plans behind his seemingly casual plotting. One sunny morning, she had rowed over to the other side of town and had just reached the bottom of the 199 steps up to St Mary's Church. She was sixteen at the time, a young woman of some standing in fine dresses, a silver pendant around her neck. She was a little odd, not only for the fact that a woman could be so apt at business, but that she would not wear a hat and instead had a length of fine silk scarf wrapped around her head as a broad headband, keeping her black tresses back from her face. She placed a gloved hand on the railing as she moved to start up to the tops of the cliffs. A couple of gentlemen were descending, and stopped as Eleanor put a foot on the first step.

The older man, head of one of the most successful ship building firms in Whitby, doffed his hat to her. "Miss Hurst," he greeted her.

Eleanor glanced up, recognising Mr Gaskin immediately. He was often at dinner when her father was in town. The two men did a lot of business together, and discussed much, eyeing up one another's empire building and business sense. Plans were made behind closed doors. Others involved were only informed on a need to know basis.

She smiled politely and gave a little bow. Whilst he was polite there was always a sense of awkwardness, of things known that could not be discussed. She never had a lot to talk about with the man and was keen to continue on her walk.

"I don't believe you've met my son," he continued, sweeping a hand out to a young man who joined him on the step, a couple ahead of Eleanor. They towered proprietarily over her. "Gerard Gaskin. My second son."

The man child, for although she knew he was just turned twenty, he still retained the chubby eagerness of a toddler, grinned down at her. Eleanor felt the temperature drop slightly as both men gazed down on her the way a farmer might examine his hens with a fine dinner on his mind. She looked uncertainly from the father to the son with the wind blown, messy hair like a jumbled auburn mop.

"This is Miss Eleanor Hurst, Mr Hobart Hurst's eldest daughter. And a very fine help in the family business she is as well."

Gerard bustled forward, bowing and taking Eleanor's hand to kiss it in a rather grand manner. He had the slobbering mouth of a fish on the market. Never had Eleanor been so glad of her gloves.

"Miss Hurst," Gerard burbled. "A fine asset to any man you must be, and a pretty one at that."

Eleanor smiled, but her facial expression did not reach her eyes. They knew something she did not. "Very nice to make your acquaintance, Mr Gaskin," she told the son, firmly pulling her hand back into her own possession. "Mr Gaskin," she nodded to father. "If you would excuse me, I am on an errand."

They nodded to her and bid her good day. It was a lie, but the moment she had seen them she had an unexplained urgency to flee their company. She would get to the top and wander the ruins of Whitby Abbey, see if she could not work out just what they were thinking. No doubt it involved her father. As she hurried up the steps, a little faster than she would have normally made herself make this ascent, she noticed the father turn to the son out of the corner of her eye. "See," he told his son. "I told you there was no reason to worry about this arrangement."

This arrangement. Eleanor felt sick as she started to get an uneasy sense of what might be going on.

During Eleanor's years in Whitby, learning household management and business, Clara enjoyed a far easier life over at the inland market town of Thirsk. This ancient settlement of ruined castle and meeting place for rural farming folk and traders lay to the west of the moorlands, and on lower ground in the Vale of Mowbray. Slow rivers, rich agricultural ground and farming characterised this land. There were corn mills and breweries, great trade in wool and linen, and all the usual industries of agricultural communities, including ironworks and blacksmiths to keep the tools of the trades going. Every Monday there was a busy market in the market place in Thirsk. At first light Clara would peer from her bedroom window in her sponsor's fine town house, and watch cattle and sheep flocks being herded into town, traders arriving with their wares on horse and cart, or by foot, and all the people of the land come to gather.

Clara had been sent to live with one of Hobart Hurst's trading partners, a certain Mr William Mowbray, of vague and distant relation to the Mowbray family who had once been seated in the castle ruins many hundreds of years ago. Mr Mowbray, a rather serious man of small spectacles and bristling sideburns was a widower, and lived in a fine townhouse with his two children and small staff to manage the house. He owned a drapers shop in Thirsk, and along with selling fabrics and other haberdashery items, provided tailoring and seamstress services. He was also a middle man for any weaving or fine embroidery worked in the area that was to be sold in the cities. With carriage stops between Edinburgh and London hitting Thirsk, it was a well connected town. The business made a tidy profit, but there were also family inheritances from both his and his late wife's family that meant the Mowbray's were able to live in distinct comfort. Mr Mowbray was considered to be one of the worthy men of local society.

When Clara, at the age of eight arrived to live with the family, and learn the more refined ways of the lady, there was only one of the children living in the home. Andrew Mowbray, at eleven and heir to the empire, was away at a boys' boarding school in York. His younger sister, Annabel, was the same age as Clara, and the two girls shared a governess. What exactly the arrangement between Mr Hurst and Mr Mowbray was, so that Clara would be housed, fed and educated, she never did learn. But then Clara rarely cared for the details. As long as people were adoring and paid her attention, she did not concern herself with the finer points. She did not miss her family to any great extent, for

Annabel was an adoring adoptive sister who was thrilled to gain a little live-in playmate. Annabel was a shy and awkward girl who did not make friends easily and spent most of her time alone. Clara found she was easy to dominate and provided enough adoration for even her young ego.

Miss Boye, the governess, was a rather plain and stern woman of some twenty years who saw to the girls' lessons in French, music, drawing, history and geography in a monotone unfulfilled way. Despite her lack of enthusiasm, she was certain that her employer got his money's worth, and would rap the girls' knuckles with a short thin stick when they did not apply themselves to their lessons. Clara was horrified that anyone should beat her, and complained to Mr Mowbray on the first evening of her punishment. He agreed with Miss Boye, and informed Clara that her father had placed her with him to ensure her good breeding and future. She should follow Miss Boye's instruction to the letter. Clara wrote to her father, pleading to be moved to a more civilised setting, but her pleas went unanswered.

Miss Boye for sometime had an air of polite satisfaction, knowing that she had won against Clara's indulgent expectations. The servants nodded to one another and gossiped in the kitchen that Miss Boye would soon enough become Mrs Mowbray. So close in confidence were the two, even if Miss Boye was almost twenty years his junior. Clara listened with narrowed eyes at the doorway.

Eight months in to her stay Clara had become a diligent student, and Miss Boye ought to have been happy, only that worry was overcoming her. At first it was only a few clumps of hair that loosened and fell out at her dressing table. It was the weather, she told herself. As the weeks progressed, she found bald patches about her head, and before Christmas time she had a shiny scalp empty of hair. She wore a mop cap to cover the absence and keep her head warm. She consulted chemists for all kinds of tonics, but none were to work. Eventually she purchased a wig which covered over her baldness for most situations, although when Mr Mowbray came upon her with her head uncovered one evening, he realised that the idea of marriage with Miss Boye would never work. She was a poor wretch who would never marry. He kept her on until the girls were sixteen, then sent her on her way with good references and little more, and within six months had married a local farmer's widow.

During the summers and at Christmas, Andrew Mowbray esquire would return to the family home, and follow his sister in blind adoration of Clara. Unknowingly it was the wisest course of action and neither child suffered from the hair loss that plagued poor Miss Boye.

When Clara was eleven a new maid of twelve years was hired to replace the previous kitchen maid who had found herself in the family way in advance of a marriage proposal that would never materialise, and hence had to go away in shame. The new maid, by the name of Mary Harker, was a sullen looking girl who had an air of misbehaviour about her. Even in the first week the cook could be heard scolding the girl for her lies, and she did not fit in well with the staff. Clara watched on from the shadows with interest.

Early one morning, as it was only just starting to dawn, Mary came out into the yard with an empty bucket. She had to fetch water from the pump for the kitchen, then she'd start on lighting the fires and waking cook up. She slumped across the yard, dragging the bucket behind her and scowling at nothing. No good person ought to be up at this time. A rustle distracted her, and she stopped, surprised to discover she was not the only person awake.

Miss Clara Hurst, the unexplainable ward of Mr Mowbray, was hunkered down on what appeared to be a little milking stool. She had a little basket with fresh eggs by her side, and a small chipped bowl in front.

"What are you doing?" Mary muttered. No doubt whatever mess was made, she would have to clean it up, and take the blame as well most likely.

"Eggs can tell us so many things," Clara said. She picked up an egg and dropped it unceremoniously into the bowl. It cracked open on impact, and Clara took a little stick to stir it around, breaking the yolk and blending in pieces of broken eggshell.

"Like messages?"

"Messages of the future."

Mary scoffed. "You got a message written on the egg shell?"

Clara smiled lightly to herself and did not meet Mary's eye. "That can sometimes be arranged. It certainly scares people. But in these broken egg shells, I can divine the future."

"Rubbish. You're putting it on. No one knows the future."

"People pay good money for this sort of thing."

The suggestion made Mary quieten in consideration. "Will you show me?"

"I can show you some things," Clara said slowly. "Although if you don't have the gift you can only go so far." She was still gently stirring the raw egg, as if stirring a pudding over the fire.

Mary lent forward and peered into the bowl. All she could see was a mess that would probably need throwing out. "What do you see in that scramble?"

Clara gave a little sigh. "A hangman's noose," she said simply before looking up and meeting Mary's eye for the first time. "You'll hang for it, Mary Harker."

Mary tittered at the prophecy. "Stuff and nonsense," she brushed it aside. "I'm away for the water."

Clara said nothing more, but smiled as she watched her new little project walk away. What plans she had for that girl.

For better or worse Clara and Eleanor were out in the world, with new towns and faces to explore and experiences to gather. For those who remained in Commondale after the breaking apart of family, life seemed to stagnate; in fact at times it was difficult to ascertain if time actually moved at all. If it were not for Stephen growing, and the increasing collection of white hairs in Maud Hurst's dark tresses, Ellen Withers wondered if they ever would have realised just how long it had been.

In the first weeks after the girls had been sent away, things were very bad. Ellen hadn't known what to do with herself, and had tried to lose her thoughts in the housework. She even took up gardening and started with some fruit bushes behind the house. She fretted over Maud, who either slept or cried and barely ate. The weight poured off her, and even little Stephen's charms seemed to be of no consolation. Maud saw no one beyond Stephen and Ellen that first month. Ellen would watch at the window, all the time hoping that Gillian would come and show her face, offer some consolation to her mother. Gossip, especially of bad news, always spread like wildfire, and there was no doubt in Ellen's mind that Gillian would have known of everything that had transpired before the day was out. But she did not come.

Mr Hodgkin, the new farm manager, soon set about reordering the business to his own ways of working, and hired a couple of lads to help him. Despite only being an employee himself, he treated everything and everyone (for there were only hired lads and women to contend with) as his private property, and soon took to strutting about the valley as if he were lord of the manner. With Maud withdrawn and locked inside her mind, she took no further interest in the farming of their land, and no longer was seen about the estate. She was not there to remind Hodgkin of his place, and increasingly he would march into the kitchen as if he were master of the house. He did not care for Stephen, who seemed too gentle a boy, and would scold and mock him in the belief that it would toughen the boy up to be a man. Instead Stephen learned to hate him with a cold fury. Ellen Withers would stand up for the boy, and for what little refuge they had in the house, but he had little respect for women, and would slap her about and tell her to watch her mouth. It continually grew worse until six months in, Maud slumped into the kitchen to find Mr Hodgkin having his way with a tearful Ellen on the kitchen table. She whacked him with a fire poker and chased him out of the house, reminding him he was a paid man and she could have him fired. He had sneered and assured them Mr Hurst wouldn't believe the word of a woman, but from then after he stayed out of Pines Lodge.

Assa, now considered part of the property's livestock, was used as a labourer and transportation. She gave Mr Hodgkin hell for the last two years of her life, and left many a hoof imprint upon various parts of his body, along with the odd broken bone, before finally succumbing to an infection. It broke Eleanor's heart when she received the letter to tell her that Assa had passed away.

Amos Cornforth did not set foot on the property again. He retreated to his little shack down in the bottom of Commondale and survived on casual labouring, moving from farm to farm as the work required it, helping with harvesting and maintenance. News and gossip travelled fast throughout the village, across the moors and down the valleys. Once again the Cornforth family's shame was discussed and heads were shaken in pity. Many agreed that Amos had been a fool to take on the post at Pines Lodge after he had been forced to sell off the property. His pride ought to have been enough to get him moving on for a fresh start whilst he was still young. He should have gone to the new world. All sorts of people sailed over there, and the opportunities and wealth were so great that one could not help but land on their feet. Instead he was in the same village, in his forties, with no wife, no proper home and only an illegitimate child to a married woman, neither of whom he could see anymore. He became wretched and saddened, and something of a charity case that first winter in his hovel, grieving over how his life had become. It did not help that everyone knew what had happened, held their own opinions on what he ought to have done, and would look at him with pity. Other people's pity is a heavy burden to carry.

The following spring, Maud, now out of her depression, made contact and appeared at his abode with news and letters. She had cleaned him up, fed him and fixed his torn shirts, and they had sat and cried together a little. She could not live to know he was so close and in such miserable circumstances, and had written to a cousin over in Haworth. There was a farming position there if he would take it, along with good lodgings. It was all far enough away for people not to have heard what had happened on the moors. He could get his life back together, and they could write at least. He did not want to go so far from his son and his love, but given that he was unable to set foot on the farm, he eventually agreed that it was probably for the best. Once the snows had melted enough, he set out on foot for the distant lands of West Riding.

The catalyst for the almighty Hurst blow up, Gillian Longbottom, nee Hurst, did not communicate with any of her family for several months. It was as if they had ceased to exist. She herself was not even certain if she was waiting for them to beg forgiveness and come to her, or if she was too frightened to approach and learn that they had disowned her forever. The first contact was a brief letter sent from Whitby, along with a belated wedding gift of linens. Stephen and Ellen saw her in the village, and Ellen told her of Maud's depression. Even then Gillian couldn't bring herself to go and see her mother. It was only the following year, when Maud had been shocked into coming back to life from Mr Hodgkin's rape of Ellen, that she went into the village and walked down by the river until she came to William's smithy. William and Gillian lived in one half of the building, the blossoming blacksmith's on the other side. With the hard labour and maturing years, for William was now in his mid twenties, he had filled out into a man, and Maud only caught glimpses of the boy she remembered chattering around his mother's skirts when she had first moved to Commondale. The first meeting was a little strained between all three, but gradually they made their peace and the residents of Pines Lodge would often go to the blacksmith's whenever they had business that took them down into the village.

Beyond Gillian's shame of the clandestine marriage and the breaking up of her birth family, she carried another horror that clung to her parasitically. With every passing month it dug its claws deeper into the back of her mind. She was not with child. At first William merely laughed and told her not to worry, these things took a little time. She was still young, they had plenty of time, and whilst they were waiting to be blessed, they could ready their home and his work for a family. With every month that her bloods came with depressing regularity, Gillian began to lose hope. She knew that William's greatest wish was a big family. That was the reason he had abandoned Megan Hammond and taken her on instead, so that the dream could still become reality. But months turned to years, his sister Mary Longbottom got married and had children with alarming regularity. Nothing came for Gillian. She grew withdrawn and saddened, unable to explain the problem. William grew distant from her, and although he did not openly admit it, she knew that his affection for her was waning as he realised he had picked a barren wife. In desperation she consulted Old Marsden for help. The old women had looked her up and down and shook her head, as if there was something upon Gillian that no herb would shake. She had made some concoction, which she said would ease Gillian's anxiety, and that was the best that could be hoped for. Gillian clung desperately to the bottle, and took it religiously, but all it did was put her into dreamless sleep at night.

After four years there were no children, and although William honoured her as his wife, he was now distant. With every commission he would travel away from home, working on particular jobs for farms and other villages. Gillian felt like a childless widow, and wondered if this was a divine punishment for having married secretly all those years ago.

There was a heady scent from beeswax candles and the whale oil in the lamps. This was mixed in with the scents of roast pork, vegetables, fruits and flowers scattered about the room, it was almost intoxicating. Outside it was dark and their glittering reflections were like paintings in the windows. Light danced upon the angles of cut glass goblets and chandeliers, the flash of cutlery as it was moved across the plate. The heat in the elegant dining room, radiating from twenty two bodies, intensified the whole experience. Eleanor felt a little light headed, and felt her corset pull at her waist. She had consumed more than enough food, and waved her hand dismissively when one of the maids went to add more food to her plate.

They were at a small gathering of select businessmen and families of the Whitby area. It was close to Eleanor's eighteenth birthday, and she was considered adult enough to be invited to such occasions. She'd never had a formal coming out into society, but had been to a few dances and social events. At such engagements most of Whitby's elite was present, but this dinner was a far more intimate affair, and certainly the prelude to something greater. She knew her father and Mr Gaskin believed her to be ignorant of their manoeuvring and empire planning. Mr Gaskin so obviously hoped it would all appear organic to her, and that somehow she would fall desperately in love with Gerard Gaskin. As to the Hob, he probably didn't care what she thought as long as she did what was expected. The old men had already proposed and accepted the offer of marriage long ago. Her participation at the end would merely be a figurehead formalisation of the agreement.

She had been left in no doubt that the son, Gerard, was more than happy with arrangements. There had been occasions when he had appeared at the Hurst office on his own, and virtually chased her around the bookkeeping desk hoping for an innocent tussle. Eleanor had managed to avoid his advances thus far, but she knew that time was getting short and she would have to find a more permanent solution soon.

Picking up her glass, she finished her wine and glanced across the table to where Gerard chortled at some joke, his lips slick with gravy sauce and his fat cheeks red with wine and the heat of the lamps. If she had to marry a man like that, she was sure she would die. She would much rather remain alone. She could work in business, set up on her own and escape the Hob, she idly fantasised.

Mrs Gaskin, a pleasant but slightly too-trusting woman of shiny, oiled skin about to flick over from youth to old age, and bouncing grey curls, leaned over to Eleanor. She had a slightly conspiratorial look about her. "Miss Hurst," she began, "I do believe you will be eighteen soon. Such a fine time to be a young woman."

Eleanor forced a smile, already knowing where this was going. The hints were getting heavier and more obvious by the day.

"Your whole life ahead of you. So much you can do. Soon the courting and marriage." She clutched onto Eleanor's wrist and shook it as if they were both to start squealing in excitement. It was all Mrs Gerard could do not to blurt out how much she was looking forward to being mother of the groom. "So much to look forward to."

"I'll be leaving Whitby soon enough." The words were out of her mouth before she had chance to consider them. Everyone's assumption that her life could be prearranged so infuriated her, worse still that they expected her to be pleased about something she did not want.

"Oh," Mrs Gaskin sounded confused, as if this wasn't part of the order of events she'd been privy too. Her clutch tentatively backed away from Eleanor's wrist.

Eleanor could feel the flash of the Hob's gaze. He was at the other end of the table but he'd heard. She didn't need to look to know he was displeased.

"I've been in Whitby four long years now."

"But Whitby is such a fine place, with such fine company," Mrs Gaskin tittered, looking pointedly at her son.

"I miss my mother. I have not seen her since I left. I am going to Commondale soon."

This appeared to confuse the woman. She was silent a moment. "Well, naturally. A girl has need of her mother, especially when she is embarking on the events of womanhood." She petted Eleanor's hand.

Events of womanhood, Eleanor thought sourly whilst keeping the smile on her face. What were those to be, exactly? Rutted by a fat greasy pig every night, and expected to keep the books for free? She still got her salary, but only because she was managing the day-to-day business. When she was shipped across to the Gaskins, she'd be well and truly part of the property and would lose any autonomy she currently enjoyed. Whilst it was true that Whitby women often dealt with money and business more than the women in other parts of the country, the Gaskins weren't a family that offered that opportunity. They were far too well off and their men did not sully their hands with such low work as fishing or whaling. With so many sailors and fishermen, it was an inevitable necessity for many families that the women became the sole head of the household for many months of the year, and had to take on the mantle for everything. The Gaskins were shipbuilders, and very rich. Any sailing and travel would be dealt with by employees. They could afford to allow their women to be kept dolls.

Hobart kept his temper under control until they were away from the party and back at his premises. He did not like anyone to take the initiative. There was a reason she had been kept away from Commondale, for as girls they had been given too much liberty and had been going wild. Look what had happened to her sister. With the more cultivated society and his watchful eye, she had been brought up as a lady, and soon enough she would make a very proper wife. So often Eleanor had taken the line of least resistance and done as bid. But she no longer saw why she should, and had spoken back. She was going to see her mother. She had every right to do so. She watched the vein throb on his forehead, before he begrudgingly conceded that it had been a while, and he would allow a week's supervised visit later in the year. For now she needed to go to bed, for there was a big shipment due tomorrow and they would be busy.

Up in her room, Eleanor packed a few essentials, her fiddle and the latest batch of letters she had written. She changed into her walking boots and put her cape on. With the saddlebag on her lap, she sat in silence and waited, watching the hands of the clock mark time. When she could hear the Hob snoring, she crept down the stairs to the kitchen. Lucy Ann was curled up asleep in her bed, dead to the world from exhaustion. She worked hard every day and fell into a soundless sleep each night. Eleanor left a letter on the kitchen table, then slipped out of the house.

Dawn was barely considering making an appearance as Eleanor walked up the river out of Whitby. Past the bobbing fishing boats, the warehouses and construction yards, the narrow leaning houses and the blubberhouses where the whale blubber was processed. Up the bank, into the trees and away from the town. It had been four years since she had last walked this route, and now that she had started upon it, she surprised herself that she hadn't left sooner. What hold did he actually have over them, other than angry words and a fast back of the hand? Perhaps this was the jump from childhood to womanhood, she considered. She no longer held the parent in awe, blindly following every command. She had certainly grown up since moving to Whitby, not just physically, but in her mind and her thoughts. The potential of life had become too much that she could accept the future selected for her.

She walked hard and steady, and did not stop to rest until she was a good way up the Esk valley, having passed Ruswarp, Sleights and Grosmont. At Egton Bridge she gave the inn a side glance, remembering it as the place where she and Hurst had eaten on the walk to Whitby. She was hungry, but decided not to stop. She wasn't sure what the Hob would do when he realised she had gone. Undoubtedly he would rant and hit things, and she hoped Lucy Ann would have enough sense to make herself scare. After the tempest, would he set out after her, or would his cunning follow another path? She was not sure.

At Danby she stopped at a farmer's cottage where the lady of the house offered her a drink of water. Eleanor had taken deliveries here back when she and Assa had been free to roam the moors, and she chatted to the woman about the locals and the news of the past few years. The women looked a little bewildered that the traveller asked after such local peculiarities, but answered politely. She never asked any questions herself, nor commented on Eleanor's absence, and it was only when Eleanor had started walking again that it occurred to her that the woman might not have realised who she was. She still looked like herself, but perhaps four years was longer than it had felt, and combined with her fine clothes, tidy hair and little hat pinned to her head, she was so out of place that people simply wouldn't make the connection back to the young girl with the donkey.

When she reached Commondale she hovered indecisively on the bridge. She knew where her sister, Gillian lived now, and she could go to visit before heading back home. She and Gillian were in contact again through letters, although there was still a touch of distance between them. On some subjects Gillian was reserved, as though she could not be open with Eleanor. Perhaps she thought that silly unmarried girls weren't capable of understanding. Eleanor didn't see things in such terms, in fact she believed her mind had broadened more, from moving away, than Gillian's which seemed to be trapped in domesticity. Life and circumstance had naturally pulled them apart.

Another day, she decided, and headed up the hill for her childhood home.

Ellen Withers looked up from the dough she was kneading on the kitchen table as someone knocked on the door. She was up to her elbows in flour, and not inclined to be dealing with visitors. She thought to shout for Stephen to answer the door, but of course he had run off to play after his luncheon. She wasn't quite sure where Maud was.

Muttering to herself, she slammed the dough down onto the table and started to brush herself down. Her eyes widened as the door started to open. What cheek some folk had inviting themselves into other people's homes like this. A fine looking young lady stepped into the kitchen. Her curled hair was a little wind tousled, as if she'd been out on the back of a cart for some time, and the bottom of her skirts were mud stained, so perhaps she'd been walking rather than riding.

"Excuse me, Miss."

The woman grinned at her.

"Oh my Lord," Ellen yelled, hobbling across as she recognised Eleanor. "You're home, my girl, you're back!" The two women hugged, Ellen feeling her eyes fill up with tears. Suddenly it was as though the banishment had only happened yesterday. They'd been kept up to date with Eleanor's news, for she wrote very long and regular letters. Hobart Hurst had been quite adamant that there were to be no visits to Whitby, and that Eleanor was very occupied in her education. They had begun to wonder if they would ever see her again.

"Why didn't you write and tell us you were coming home?"

Eleanor winced. "This wasn't planned."

Ellen caught a look in her eye. "Does he know?"

She shook her head.

"Oh Lord, will we have his wrath coming down on us?"

"I hope not."

"Whose wrath?" Maud appeared in the doorway. She could see Ellen talking to someone, but the woman's back was to her, and from those fine dresses, Maud couldn't think it was anyone from the village. "We have a visitor, Ellen?"

Eleanor had been taking her hat off. She pushed the hat pin back through the hat and tossed it down onto the table, disregarding the flour. "Mama," she turned and broke into a tearful smile.

Maud regarded her blankly for a moment. "My girl," she whispered. "Eleanor, have you really come back to us?"

"Not with her father's blessing," Ellen muttered as mother and daughter hugged. "You sneak off in the middle of the night, Eleanor?"

"No matter," Maud said. "I'm just glad to have you home. It's been too long."

It was five days before the letter arrived at the house. Every day the women had alternated between joy at being together again, and dread whenever they heard a footstep outside. Was this Hobart returned to tear them apart? Instead it was not his person but his penned message to inform them of how things would be. Eleanor sat in the kitchen window and read it whilst her mother and Ellen hovered, wanting to know what he had decreed.

"It seems he's mellowing in his old age," Eleanor commented, offering the letter out to them to read.

Ellen shook out her apron. "You know we don't read too good."

"Tell us what he says," Maud added. She read slowly and wanted to know quicker than she would get through Hobart's particularly spidery hand.

"He says his anger has calmed, and he now understands that I have missed my mother. It is a good thing I have come home to see you all and I may stay for the summer. Then I will return to

Whitby to continue as planned, for all the arrangements have been made."

"Arrangements?"

Eleanor pulled a face and looked out of the window. "I'm to be married."

Ellen started clapping in joy until Maud gave her a sharp look. "Is this not what you wish?"

"Absolutely not," Eleanor muttered. "Aside from the fact that this has all been agreed without anyone even needing to ask my opinion or even propose to me."

"We are women," Maud sighed. "Our fates are not our own."

"But that's not fair."

"This is the world."

"He's a pig," she hissed. "Even if I had been given the choice, I would have said no. I feel quite sick when I catch sight of him."

Ellen sniffed. "How many times have I heard a wife say that?"

Maud hushed her and went to sit with Eleanor. "We are women, what can we do? We are at the mercy of his charity. We can't run away and set up home ourselves."

"I might just do that," Eleanor muttered. "Besides, I have the summer to think of something."

"We'll all think of something," Ellen decided. "He's bullied us all enough already."

"I know, I just don't see what we can do."

Eleanor narrowed her eyes. She couldn't think of anything either, but there had to be something. She would go up and see Atheleys, visit her friends over at Chequers. Somewhere there would be the idea, just waiting for her to take it.

A week later found Eleanor walking across the moors to Chequers for the first time in four years. She had a bag with the letters and things she had meant to send before her impromptu departure from Whitby. In some respects it was as though the time had never passed, and Eleanor was a girl again, skipping through the sunshine. Yet there were signs that life was moving on. Saplings had rushed up to the sky and were starting to resemble adult trees. Assa was no longer with her, and it was strange not doing this walk with Assa. She felt the old donkey's loss fresh, even though she had passed on two years ago.

Chequers was much as she remembered, a faithful steadfast, with only minor changes such as a fresh coat of paint on the front door. She entered the inn, setting her bag down on an empty table. It was only the early afternoon and customers would still be travelling or out walking. Unsheathing her hat pin like a dagger, she removed her hat and poked the pin back into the brim of the hat for safekeeping.

Mrs Barker bustled into the room, jumping when she saw the lady close to the door. "Afternoon Miss," she greeted the stranger as she replenished her shelves with clean tankards. "I hadn't realised we had custom in the inn so early."

Eleanor rolled her eyes. She couldn't believe she was that changed or forgotten. She remembered everyone and no one had aged that much in four years as to have become a stranger. "Mrs Barker," she scolded. "Don't tell me you don't know me. Especially when I've come over with things to deliver for you."

Mrs Baker stopped in her work and gave the young woman a proper examination. "Miss Hurst," she broke out, grinning widely.

She took a few steps towards Eleanor before changing direction and heading for the doorway to the rest of the property. "Anna," she yelled for the maid. "Miss Hurst is returned, come through here now!"

"I've brought all the letters and things I meant to send."

"This not a planned visit?" Mrs Barker hurried over to hug her.

"It was an impulsive move back to Commondale," Eleanor admitted, laughing. "I realised I had been trapped in Whitby too long."

"Well, you're a breath of fresh air," Mrs Barker agreed, holding her back at arm's length. "Just look at you, what a fine lady you've grown up into."

"Eleanor Hurst." Anna, last seen as a young kitchen maid, had grown up at a similar pace to Eleanor. Absence had actually allowed the two girls to become close through their letters, Anna being surprisingly literate for a working girl, and they had sent many gifts to one another, Anna being the provider of many a fine embroidered item. "And look at this beautiful dress. Whitby has most certainly agreed with you."

"And I'll wager a fine woman as this must be engaged by now," Mrs Barker chortled, winking at Eleanor knowingly. "I'm sure every young man in Whitby has his head turned. Tell me, are you playing them for a batch of fools, or have you already made your choice."

Eleanor shook her head. What naive times they lived in, as if she had a choice in the matter. "I am not attached to anyone." The Hob would have disagreed, but as no one had ever proposed to Eleanor, and thus she had never been given the opportunity to accept or decline, she considered herself a fully unattached woman.

Mrs Barker patted her shoulder. "I doubt you'll stay that way for long. Do you still play that fiddle as well as you used to?"

"Better I'd like to think."

"Marvellous. We're sorting laundry out the back in the garden, for it is such a fine day. Come out and play for us. And make it a fast jig. It should make us get a move on."

Eleanor sat on the drystone wall surrounding the garden and played for the two women as they got on with the task of taking down all the dry sheets and table cloths from the lines. Later cattle began to be herded into the surrounding grazing meadows as a group of drovers arrived for a night's rest. Eleanor moved down to the front of the property, finding a new perch upon the stone wall and watched the men work with the beasts whilst she idly played the fiddle. A number of faces she recognised, others she did not. Cameron MacCaskill was there, and gave her a wordless friendly nod. When the old Scot was working, he did not like to waste words. She smiled back at him. It was good to see some of the old crowd, although she would have rather caught up with her dear friend Angus. He'd been working other droving routes the past couple of years and the last she had heard from him, it had been doubtful he'd set foot in Yorkshire at all this year.

When the cattle were safely penned in, one of the Scots shouted at Eleanor to play something a bit more lively. She started off into her repertoire of Scottish jigs, to the whooped delight of the men. Some started to dance, and with a shortage of women, were not too abashed to take one another as partners as they danced off their spare energy out on the flatter grass just in front of Chequers. Anna was pulled away from her work and caught up in the swirling dance, sunlight bounding from her hair as her mop cap fell off. She was laughing so hard she could barely keep track of her feet.

Eleanor slipped down off the stone wall, the notes faltering as she stumbled down the grassy slope. With a fiddle under her chin and the bow slicing back and forth, she could hardly dance with a partner, but instead she swirled in and around the dancers, feeling her blood rush through her body. This was far greater than any formal dinner party making polite conversation across the soup bowl and watching the men get drunker and greasier as the night wore on.

"Miss Eleanor Hurst, I didn't ken you from any other stranger the now," a voice close by burst out. Eleanor stumbled as she was swept around in a dance, her fiddle coming free from her chin. She held on to it by the neck along with the bow, but the music abruptly stopped.

It took a moment to make sense of the man's face before her, for in four years he had broadened out from a young man to a man. With a wide grin she gave up any thought of playing and flung her arms around his neck, much to his surprise at such close contact. "Angus MacCaskill, you told me you weren't coming to Yorkshire this year."

One of the other Scots came up behind Angus and gave Eleanor a knowing look. "I'll just be borrowing your fiddle the now," he said, taking the instrument from Eleanor. "We can't dance without a wee bit of music."

"It's so good to see you."

"Aye, you too."

They were jostled amongst the other dancers as the music started up again.

Angus took her hand. "Come and talk with me."

The two of them slipped out of the bustle, ignoring the knowing nods and laughter. One of the men called over to Angus; "You two away to a room now?"

"We'll be conversing like gentlefolk out here in front of the inn."

There was a bench set in front of the walls of the Chequers property, which they commandeered for the next couple of hours, to talk through everything they had written to one another over the past four years, and things that had not been mentioned. Both parties kept some thoughts and events back, a little uncertain of things now that they had found each other quite grown up. Angus still had his shaggy locks and slight ambience of chaos, although he had broadened out to fill his overcoat, and had a steady maturity about him. It was only by seeing him again that Eleanor realised how much she had missed their meetings, however sparse, these past years. It felt as though something crucial, forgotten in a lapse of memory, and been returned to her, and she felt right again. She almost wanted to weep with joy at the reunion, but held back her emotions lest he think she had grown up into a silly emotional wretch, and would not wish to socialise with her any longer.

In the droving world Angus had now come of age. At thirty, as he had told her in the past, a man was then old enough to apply for his droving licence. Eleanor pestered him to show her the licence, which he did eventually, taking the handwritten licence out of his overcoat pocket. Such a novelty it was, that he was keeping it neat and fresh by hiding it away a lot of the time. He had only turned thirty early this year, and had not had the licence that long. There was an odd sense of melancholy as they talked of him getting his licence, as if it held regret for him. Eleanor couldn't understand it, and once the document had been examined, they swiftly moved on to other subjects.

As the evening wore on the dancers moved into the inn for their food and drink, a chance to sit and talk, tap their feet to the music as the fiddle was passed around those who could play. Eleanor and Angus remained outside. Eventually they got up and took a slow amble back up the droving route, Angus walking along the track, Eleanor up on the grassy line hump built up against cartwheel ruts. They were almost the same height now.

"Whitby is agreeing with you," Angus started. "That is to say you look very well for it. You mean to settle there permanently?"

Eleanor pulled a face. "No. Of course, it is a nice place to live and I have no grievance with the town itself..."

They stopped walking. Eleanor stared down at the grass springing up around her shoes. She hadn't told Angus anything of the Gaskins in her letters. Consciously it had been the obvious thing to neglect mentioning, although she was not completely sure of her motivation. Only that there was a fear she might not have heard from him again.

Angus watched her, feeling uneasy now. "Is there a problem in Whitby? No one's been threatening you?"

She shook her head. "No, not as such. I'm not in any danger." She caught his eye. He looked very worried. She exhaled deeply. "The truth is my father wants me to marry the son of one of his business contacts there. I think if I had not forced the need to come back to Commondale to visit my mother, he would have me married away by now."

"Oh." Angus took a step back from her as if she was infectious.

Eleanor unconsciously toyed with the thistle pendant about her neck. "My issue is that I have no desire to marry this man. He is not all that pleasant and even the mere sight of him is averse. It does not seem like a good basis for marriage. The thought that it may be the rest of my life..." she broke off. There was a waver in her voice. Because she knew this was a very real possibility, and it was rushing up to her with alarming speed. "I have been trying to think of a way to escape it, but all I have come up with is running away to some far place. Which would be all well and good for a couple of days, but as to the practicalities of the rest of my life, I do not know how it would work. I'm afraid all I have are fanciful solutions that would not work in the real world."

She felt her eyes filling up with tears and coughed quickly to push down the feeling of panic. She slapped at the top of her legs as if to say, well, enough of this nonsense. "Oh Angus, if only I could run away and marry you." It came out as a flippant comment, but as soon as the words were out, she realised she would have been thrilled with such an outcome.

Angus looked pained. "Eleanor, I wish that I..." he never finished the thought. Instead he stepped up to her, and catching a hand around her lower back, kissed her. It was the first time anyone had kissed her beyond the motherly pecks of her Mama and Ellen, and happy toddler slobberings from Stephen. It took her by surprise and Eleanor felt herself loose her balance. She clung on to his coat collar to right herself, then with her centre regained felt that this was what she had been waiting for. She kissed him back and let her fingers move up through those tangled locks.

They stumbled backwards off the track and into the heather as the light began to fade from the sky, the sun growing heavy and sinking towards the hills to rest in darkness. Without thought his overcoat was off and spread into a gap between the heather, and Eleanor had sunk onto her back, pulling him down with her and quite sure she never wanted to let him go again. Clothes were loosened, belts and buckles undone with an animal urgency and they were soon together with a haste and urgency as though this had been long overdue for centuries. Eleanor had not given herself a moment to think before it was over, and she was surprised that it was not as she had expected. She had overheard women laughing about their first times with men, mostly the married women, but a lot of the serving girls in Whitby didn't wait for the nuptials of the church. So many said it hurt, or it was over in a flash, or that they'd barely noticed, they'd laughed coarsely. Some had mentioned blood. It had been a strange sensation that made her cry out, but it had not been agony, and there was no bleeding afterwards. She supposed these things were different for everyone.

Afterwards, with breeches up and skirts brushed down, they lay back in the heather and gazed up at the darkening sky. Angus put a hand over his eyes. "I should not have done that."

Eleanor rolled to her side and pulled his hand to her. "Why not? I wanted you to."

"Drovers are supposed to be trustworthy men of virtue. That's why we have to meet the criteria..."

"Turn thirty?"

He avoided the comment. "We shouldn't be taking advantage of young women along the droving road."

"I was just as willing as you. I'd hardly call it taking advantage. Besides, are you telling me you do this at every inn you stop at?"

"No." He looked at her earnestly. "Eleanor, I have loved you for many a year, I've just never found the right way to tell you."

She stretched up against the line of his body and kissed him, feeling his arms move around her frame.

"I have to go tomorrow. We're away to London with these cattle."

"I am going to see you again? You'll come back to me? You know I'm at Commondale; it's not far from here."

"You'll be away to marry your Whitby merchant."

"Not whilst you exist in the world."

They remained coiled in silence.

"Angus, you will come back for me, won't you?" she whispered.

He paused. "Aye, I will," he said, coming to a decision. "Just as soon as I can."

It was quite normal that Hobart Hurst would never let a household know when to expect him. This summer was no exception and Pines Lodge holding its breath every time they saw a figure crossing the moors, a change in the air or a tap on the door. Eleanor tried to relax, but carried an underlying unease, wondering when he would appear and try to force her back to Whitby. Between waiting for Angus and hoping she would not see her father, her days were spent with one eye looking over her shoulder.

She did not confide in anyone. No one, not Ellen nor Maud and probably Stephen either were under any illusion as to how she felt about the patriarch. Yet as the months passed Eleanor received less sympathy from her family, in particular Ellen Withers, who was increasingly suspicious that she was up to something. In the height of summer Eleanor became ill and listless and did not keep much food down. Many times she found herself rushing out to the yard to heave the meagre contents of her stomach into a bucket.

On one morning when the retching was finished and she raised her head, she discovered Ellen Withers at the back door. Her arms were folded and she was staring down at Eleanor with impatience.

"Just remind me again why you had to go dashing off from Whitby."

"I already told you."

"Tell me again."

Eleanor sat back on her haunches. "It had been four years since I last saw you all. I thought you were pleased to have me."

"Stop avoiding the point. Why now?"

"He was going to force me to marry."

"Oh aye,"

"You saw the letter. I've told you everything."

"And why must you marry?"

"To establish permanent links to strengthen his business empire."

Ellen raised a single eyebrow. "Is that what we're calling it these days? Watch yourself, girl," she advised as she headed back into the house. "Your mother's covering her eyes for now, but there'll come a point where there's no denying it."

Eleanor scowled at the farmhouse in confusion, then stuck her tongue out in irritation. Struggling up to her feet, she smoothed her skirts, then picked up the bucket with her vomit and went to swill it out. She considered going back into the house to have it out with Ellen, and clear up whatever nonsense the woman had stuck in her mind, but felt her courage weaken and took to the moors instead.

Atheleys was waiting at their usual mound, as if she had known Eleanor would be arriving shortly. They never made any particular arrangement to meet. The past three months had been blissfully reminiscent of childhood, meeting virtually every day and talking of anything and everything.

Humming quietly, Atheleys was weaving herself a little ring of blooming heather to put upon her head. She had taken her hair out of its usual plaits and brushed it. The silvery blonde lengths swept out gently on the breeze. She looked up as Eleanor approached and lowered her moorland crown. "You look as sick as a pig."

"I have some ailment," Eleanor sighed as she slumped down in the heather. "It's taking some shifting."

Atheleys snorted.

"Ellen Withers is behaving as though I am a criminal."

"In some people's eyes you probably are."

"I haven't done anything wrong."

"Don't you know what's wrong with you?" she asked incredulously. "It ought to be as clear as the nose on your face." She leaned into her friend, popping the heather ring on her head in a jovial manner. "Don't you know about the laws of nature?"

"I understand nature better than most."

"You do know how women get their babies, don't you?"

Eleanor stared at her, a little mortified that she would think her so naive. "I grew up on a farm. I know about rutting. I'm not some fine little lady living in the town and sheltered in ignorance till her wedding night."

"So you know you're with child, don't you?"

"I am not."

"Are you going to tell me you're still an innocent maid, Eleanor?" Atheleys took back her heather ring. There was silence, and she gave a knowing look as Eleanor averted her gaze and looked at her feet.

"I'm not," Eleanor started quietly. "But it was only the once and I'm not married."

Atheleys laughed. "You have a poor understanding of what is and isn't required in states of life if you think a girl needs to be married to get herself a child. I know you're with child, and you know it too, although you daren't admit it. It's been three months gone now. You're going to feel it soon. Then you'll get fat. And then your Whitby pig won't want you anyway."

"Oh God," Eleanor groaned, closing her eyes. Angus, she thought to no one but herself. You have to come to me. I don't know what I am going to do without you.

"Don't worry," Atheleys smiled, giving her shoulders a squeeze. "I'm really looking forward to it."

Unfortunately for Eleanor, of the women she knew in Commondale, Atheleys' reaction was by far the most positive.

When Maud and Ellen finally had it out with her in the kitchen, Maud sat at the table and sobbed. Ellen was furious. Eleanor sat at the head of the table, feeling as though she was being reprimanded by both parents, a family unit.

Maud looked at her daughter sadly. "I didn't want you to have the same life I did."

"I've not lived the same life as you."

"You stupid little girl," Ellen scolded. "Out of all the children I always thought you were the most sensible. The others, out of idiocy or overtly romantic intentions, were always bound to get themselves into predicaments. But not our Eleanor, she's far too clever and talented. Just look at her running her little delivery business. She wouldn't let some man have his way with her."

"He's not some man," Eleanor muttered.

"Oh, well at least it sounds like you know who the father is."

"What do you think of me?" Eleanor shrieked. "I am not some tart who changes her men every week."

"Tart!" Ellen laughed. "Get used to it girl for they'll be calling you worse than that. A woman with child who isn't married. She needs to sort herself out pronto, you understand. I suppose we'll need to write to this man in Whitby, get him up here forthwith and you to the altar. You're barely showing so it could be respectable."

Eleanor had a flash of a sickening alternate life, where somehow she had been seduced into Gerard Gaskin's bed far in advance of any marriage. As a result she had carried a little pig in her belly. "It's not Gaskin's. I cannot stand the man."

Ellen scowled at her and turned her back to vent her fury on whatever was boiling in the pot. "He won't like that. Your father's planned out the future for all you children. You saw how mad he got over Gillian..."

"Ellen," Maud spoke quietly, advising her maid to be quiet. Sometimes she did overstep the mark. She looked to Eleanor. "Who is he?"

Eleanor ran her thumbnail into the kitchen table. "His name is Angus MacCaskill."

"A Scot?"

She nodded.

"And how long have you known him?"

"Years. He's one of the drovers. They pass through Chequers and..."

Ellen couldn't help herself. "A drover! I bet he has a girl like you in every county."

"Drovers are honourable men, and he wouldn't do that," Eleanor declared with blind adoration. "They don't just give droving licences to anyone. You have to meet the criteria. Anyway, he's coming back here, to Commondale. He promised."

"Does he know you're with child?"

Eleanor slumped back in her chair. "No. But he's going to come back and marry me." The lack of a proposal for any marriage didn't occur to Eleanor. The Hob had arranged for her to marry Gerard Gaskin, but there had never been a proposal, merely an understanding. Ergo the same could be applied to Angus. They loved each other, he had promised to come back. As soon as he knew there was a baby on the way, he'd marry her. She had no doubt.

Gillian reacted the worst out of the family. If Eleanor had hoped on sisterly solidarity, she had been a fool. Gillian had become withdrawn and fuelled by seething anger over the years, just waiting for the right spark to set her off. She had come up to the farm on one of her sparse visits, and had been quietly informed of the events by her mother. Her fingers balled up into fists and she marched off to find her twin. Eleanor was a short way from the farm, sat in the heather eating honey out of a small pot with her fingers like a child. Gillian looked disdainfully on her sister, with her pretty dresses, now straining at the waist, and jewellery about her neck. So this was the height of sophistication, was it, getting with child out of wedlock?

"Mama says you're expecting."

Eleanor jumped. So engrossed she had been in her honey, she'd not heard Gillian thunder up the hill.

"Gillian," she started, putting the honey pot aside and looking for something to wipe her sticky fingers on. With nothing to hand, she quickly sucked the residue off her fingers, which brought forth an even colder stare from her twin. "I feel like I haven't seen you for weeks."

"You haven't," Gillian snapped. "So is it true?"

"Yes, it's true."

"And you're not married."

"Not yet."

Gillian laughed coldly. "I bet he won't want you now."

"Yes he will."

There was a silent stand off between the two. The air felt chilled despite the sunshine. Gillian shook her head in disgust. "It is a great sin what you've done. How could you?"

"We're in love..."

"You've done this to spite me."

"What?"

"You're not married, you shouldn't be having children."

"But this has nothing to do with you."

Gillian's eyes were filling up with tears. "I've been married four years and I ought to have two little ones and another on the way by now. But I have nothing. I have been good. I have gone to church. I got married first. And you, you just spread your legs for some passing..."

"Don't speak to me like that."

Gillian pushed at her sister. Eleanor lost her balance, her skirts billowing out as she fell on her rear end, the bushy heather cushioning her fall. "You are an immoral whore of the devil," she shrieked. "And you do this to mock me. May you burn in hell for your sins, Eleanor Hurst. You are not my sister."

Eleanor, who had been more emotional of late, burst into tears as her sister left her in a tangle in the heather. Gillian marched down the hill without looking back, and returned home in a filthy mood. Eleanor stayed up in the heather for a long time. Ellen had warned her that people would call her worse than tart, but she had never thought the worst would come from her own sister.

When the Hob arrived at Pines Lodge to take Eleanor back to Whitby, she was six months pregnant, and there was no hiding that bump she carried. No one needed to explain to him what had happened. Maud was in a chair knitting, and Ellen was out in the village with little Stephen. Mr Hodgkin had left the day previous to attend an annual sheep market and would be gone for some days. Eleanor was cooking soup. Hobart stepped into the kitchen, saw Eleanor with her hands on her back, stretching by the fire, and realised in that moment that the union with the Gaskins was over.

"I thought I was doing you a kindness by allowing half a year with your mother before your marriage to Gerard Gaskin."

"A marriage no one thought to mention to me?" Eleanor stepped up to the table. She had been so frightened of facing the Hob over this. Now that he was here she was angry, full of fury against the way the world was ordered. She was not going to whimper and beg for his forgiveness."

"You knew the score. You're clever enough to have inferred it. But instead you come back here and it all goes to ruin. I said it before, all those years when that stupid sister of yours got married without permission. This place is no place to raise girls." He turned on Maud. "You are an incompetent mother..."

"Hobart..." Maud started. She was visibly shaking.

"I shouldn't have expected any better, considering the stock you come from."

"From you?"

He spat in Eleanor's direction. "Don't talk back to me, whore. You are not of my seed. You're no better than your pathetic whore of a mother. I should not have expected anything more of you. What did he tell you? That he loved you and that he'd be back for you? I don't see a ring on your finger." He stepped around the table and grabbed at Eleanor's arm, pulling her across the room. Maud cried out and jumped from her seat, pulling at her husband's free arm.

"He does love me."

"Not only a whore but a fool."

"Hobart, leave her be."

He pushed his wife to the floor. "I don't suppose I can hope to be so lucky as this is Gerard's work?" The expression on Eleanor's face was all the answer he needed. "So which knight on shining armour has done this? Has he run away to another farm rather than face up to his duties?"

"He's away just now, but he'll come any day," Eleanor insisted. As the weeks had gone by a chink in her certainty had begun to form. Her doubts were not something she was prepared to voice yet, and certainly not to her father. "He's a drover..."

"A drover? My God girl, you do know how to pick them," he said, shaking her furiously.

"Drovers are upstanding members of the community," Eleanor started, trying to pull herself free from his grip. He was an old man, already in his sixties, yet his strength was immense. "He has his licence as well."

This seemed to amuse Hobart, and he flung her down into a seat. "He has his licence and you think you'll see him again?"

"They don't give licences to just anyone. You have to meet the criteria."

"I know that full well."

"You have to be thirty, so he's no foolish boy."

"And?"

"And what?"

"What else do they have to be?" He leered down at her.

Eleanor hadn't the faintest idea. They had never talked of the requirements or process in procuring a licence. "I would assume one would need to know the rules of a drover..."

"Stop talking such drivel. I thought I had educated you better than this, to understand the world and to be a judge of a man's character." He straightened. "I can see that I was mistaken. I was foolish. One can't expect much of a whore's daughter."

Eleanor looked from Hobart to her mother, who was sobbing on the floor. So she was not his flesh and blood. Of that she was glad.

Hobart put his hands on the arms of the chair Eleanor sat on, and leaned into her face. "Don't you know what a man has to do to get a droving licence? He has to be thirty. He has to own his own property..."

"Well, then I'll have somewhere to live..."

"And he must be married."

Eleanor fell dumbly silent.

Hobart stepped back from her chair, laughing without humour. "Did he neglect to mention that he already has a wife?" Stupid child. How was he going to explain this one to the Gaskins? Not only would it spoil their plans, but it would anger the Gaskins, make them more apt to do something foolish in revenge. Cancel a contract. Work with the competition. They would all lose out financially. "So tell me, was it worth it?"

Eleanor didn't hear him. Angus was already married? Certainly he'd never said the actual words to her, never mentioned marriage or weddings, but she'd just assumed that when he said he'd be back for her, that was what he meant. When he saw that she was expecting his child, of course he'd want to marry her. Even if she wasn't pregnant, he would still want her, for he had professed his love to her. She felt a howling anguish come up from the pit of her stomach.

Hobart slapped her firmly around the face. "Answer me now, you little bitch."

As if just waking from slumber, tears from a nightmare fresh in her eyes, Eleanor looked slowly up at him. It was not quick enough, and he grabbed at her wrist, wrenching her out of the chair and throwing her across the room. Eleanor collided with the carved wooden post near the fire and knocked her head. Her vision blurred for a moment and her sense of time paused. She slumped down to her knees, trying to recall how she had come to be by the kitchen fire. Hobart stepped over to her, took a fistful of her hair which made her scream, and threw her fully across the floor.

Maud pulled herself up to her feet and threw herself at her husband. Hobart picked up his walking stick and swung it around to whack his wife neatly on the back of her skull. Maud blacked out and dropped to the floor like a rag. He returned to his sobbing adoptive daughter and hit her across the shoulders with his stick. Did she have any comprehension of the trouble she had caused?

"I heard no talk of your pregnancy in the village," he said as he leaned over her. "Perhaps this can be salvaged. Let's see if we can't get this little bastard out of you now." And with that thought he gave her a great kick to the stomach. Eleanor groaned and felt her body automatically curl up around his foot. Her breathes escaped her body as rasps. Her eyes gummed together with tears.

"Not enough?" The hob roared. "Let's try it again then."

The second kick hit Eleanor like a cannonball and she screamed. Her body lurched internally in response. There was a feeling of a downward push as if her very being wished to vacate itself. Her stomach contracted and she scrambled onto her hands and knees as the vomit came regurgitating up in unsteady waves. She could hear the Hob pacing like a boxer waiting for his opponent to get up for the next round. Unsteadily she sat up and held out a hand. "Please."

He swung a punch and met her on the side of the head. She tumbled into the table then slipped slickly to the floor. A hot gush burst on her face and a fountain of blood poured from her nose. She wiped at her eyes and felt the blood slick on the back of her hand. She had broken out into a heavy sweat and felt woozy. Splattered vomit smeared into her skirts. Her hair had been pulled out of fashion and was hanging around her bloodied face.

"What have you got to say for yourself now?" he screamed at her.

It was at this point that Ellen Withers returned to the farm. She and Stephen heard the screaming out on the yard. Stephen clutched at Ellen's hand and looked fearfully up at her. She glanced down at the boy. He was lucky enough to have missed the worst of Hurst's tempers. She felt her ankle start to throb. "Go hide in the barn," she whispered to the boy. "And don't come out until one of us fetches you."

With Stephen out of punching distance, Ellen hobbled across the yard and wrenched the door open, terrified of what she was going to find. Inside Maud was passed out cold on the floor. Near the fire Hobart was holding a bloodied Eleanor up. The girl sported a growing bruise at her left eye and a dripping bloody nose. Her hair was tussled and wrenched, her dress ripped. There was blood and vomit on the floor. Ellen looked from the washings of blood to Eleanor's face, and realised it was more than just the nose. There was a growing slick, wet stain on the girl's dress.

The intrusion broke Hobart's intention, and he let go of Eleanor to look around to the door. As woozy as Eleanor was, she was sharp enough to take her chance, and fled from the kitchen, rushing out the back of the farm. Tripping over the bucket in the half light as dusk was falling, she cried out as she hit the earth, grazing the palms of her hands as she landed. She staggered and lurched back up, running out of the yard as Hobart burst forth from the farmhouse.

"Get off my property," he screamed at her retreating figure. "And don't come back until the bastard's dead and you're repentant of your sins."

Eleanor ran off into the dark. Her vision was blurred from the tears and the light was poor. She could not see a thing. She had spent so much time on these hills that she could have found her way blindfolded, and it was a lucky thing that night. She tripped and ran down to the little beck, then up the other side of the hill, away from the farm, away from the village, and further out into open moorland. She was crying desperately aloud, unable to think, only conscious of the simple fact that she had to get away.

She managed to get a surprising distance before the contractions in her belly became too much and she had to stumble off the path and into the heather. It felt as though the very flesh of her was being wrenched up from inside her hips. Falling to her hands and feet, crying desperately, she pressed her face into the rough scratching body of the heather. She groaned in agony as her body contracted in on itself again. Her hand went to her lower abdomen, and returned shaking and covered in the blood that had soaked through her skirts. Eleanor was no midwife nor experienced childbearing woman, but she knew that this was not good. It was far too early for her time.

Her terror was interrupted as it felt as though her body was trying to compress itself into half the length and she screamed. It was an animal roar, deeper than human thought and consciousness, down into the basic roots of pain. She could not do this. Her arms were shaking uncontrollably and she did not have the strength to hold herself up on all fours. She was going to die out here on the moors in the dark. It didn't matter. He had lied to her. He was already married. Now that the Hob had said it, she knew it was true. Men had to be married to get their licence. She had been such an idiot. Her chest contracted in on itself as if her heart were disintegrating. Let me die now, she thought.

"Eleanor." The whisper appeared by her ear, nervous and anxious. Eleanor groaned, and weakened, falling to her side as if to slump over in the heather. A way marker stone she hadn't noticed stopped her fall and propped her up by her right shoulder.

"Eleanor," the little voice repeated, and she felt cool hands on her forehead, brushing the loose hair off her sweat laden forehead.

She forced her eyes open and looked into the twilight. Atheleys stared anxiously back at her. She was hunched down in the heather beside her friend, gently patting her shoulder and looking as though she was at a loss as to what was to be done.

"What has happened?"

"He beat me."

"The Hob?"

"It's coming now."

"Your child?"

"I'm going to die out here."

Atheleys put a hand to Eleanor's head. "I will help you."

They remained hunkered down in the heather through the night, the loudest of the nocturnal creatures on the moorland that night. Grouse nestled into the depths of the heather, hearing the unfamiliar groans, and choosing to keep far away from the pained creature that made such sounds. Sheep raised their heads and looked to the sky, before lowering again to return to slumber. Every beast had to suffer alone, and if they could not break through the pain, it was nature's way that death would come.

Atheleys quietly fussed about Eleanor. When the time came for her body to finally expunge the contents of the womb, Atheleys took off a couple of her ragged little shawls and caught the tiny baby as it slipped free of Eleanor. She stroked Eleanor's back, looking down at the crumpled little face, all screwed up as if furious or struggling to digest its dinner. The bloodied cord ran back into Eleanor.

"You have to push once more, there's something else to come out," Atheleys said. "I've seen it with the sheep."

With a fading scream the afterbirth was out. Atheleys wrapped it up in a rag and put it to one side. Eleanor shuddered and flopped down into the heather, utterly spent. Birds chirped at the dawn chorus. The start of another bright day. Eleanor just wanted to die.

"It's dead, isn't it?"

Atheleys looked up from the little face. "Yes," she whispered. She crept up to Eleanor and held the little creature out for her to see. "I'm so sorry."

Eleanor started to cry. "It was too early. It was months too early."

"Too small to live in your world," Atheleys tenderly cradled the little bundle. Taking a corner of the shawl, she wiped the blood from the little boy's face. "But not for me." She leaned forward, grasping Eleanor's shoulder. "Oh let me keep him, Eleanor, please. I'll take ever such good care of him."

"He's dead."

"But with me, he might live. I mean, if I take him back to my home." She glanced back to check where she had left the afterbirth, carefully bundled in a rag. If she buried that in her mound, there was a chance he'd be able to live with her. "He was never meant to survive in your world, but you know I'm not like you." She held Eleanor's gaze. If only she'd grant her this gift.

Eleanor reached out and stroked the dead child's cheek. "And he'd live with you?"

Atheleys nodded eagerly.

"Some good might as well come of this."

Atheleys clapped in delight, holding the baby to her chest. "Oh thank you, Eleanor. You can't imagine what this means to me. You just rest here and I'll be back shortly." Gathering up the bundled afterbirth, she scuttled off across the moors.

Eleanor sank deeper into the heather. She'd heard stories of babies being switched with changelings by the little folk. All fairy stories apparently. But some talked of the hobgoblins as if they were still real. Living out in nature, coming to humans to help out now and then or cause mischief. Was a mother supposed to give up her child so easily, she wondered. Her child had been still born, months too early. Dead on arrival. She closed her eyes. She'd had such hopes but a day ago, and now she had never felt quite so alone. Utterly desolate.

She must have drifted off, for she woke to the sound of Atheleys' chatter. She had returned with armloads of sphagnum moss that she had gathered from a boggy patch close to her own little mound. "Forgive the intimacy," she said as she rolled up Eleanor's skirts. "But you're bleeding dreadfully. We must pack you with this. It will help you heal."

For the day Eleanor lay in the heather with her head in Atheleys' lap, and drifted in and of sleep. Atheleys chattered on about the moors and the landscape. Where Eleanor might find her, where her own little mound stood. She talked of the other mounds, now abandoned by old hobs long since passed, and how there was only Atheleys left on this stretch of moorland. The stories and descriptions filtered through Eleanor's mind like half imagined dreams, and her body rested. Atheleys kept a damp piece of moss on Eleanor's eye, where Hobart had hit her, to take away the worst of the swelling. Skylarks sang overhead. The clucking of grouse sounded on the horizon. Atheleys watched a hen harrier drift over the moorland, its beady eyes ever searching for the next meal. The sun warmed breeze washed over them and diluted the pain.

At early evening, as it started to grow dark again, Eleanor sat up.

"How are you?"

Eleanor looked about her. "Almost as if it were all a dream. But it's not, is it?" She looked over at Atheleys. "He's dead, isn't he?"

"He'll live at my mound, but he won't be able to come back to your world."

She felt the tender skin around her eye. It was not as bad as she had feared. She'd seen sailors in Whitby who'd gotten into fights, and afterwards the skin had swelled so much that they could not open their eye. At least she could still see.

"What will you do?"

"I suppose I should go back. I don't want to. He'll still be there, won't he? And now that I don't have a child, he'll take me back to Whitby and force me to marry that pig. I don't think I could take another beating." She felt herself crying again. Surely she was barren of tears by now.

"What about the father? There must have been a man..."

"He's married," Eleanor interrupted. She didn't want to hear helpful suggestions that could never be. "He's already married. He said he loved me, that he's loved me, but clearly not enough to keep him from her. He was never coming back for me. I've been such an idiot. I don't know what to do. There's nothing good ahead. He'll make my life a misery."

"The Hob?"

Eleanor nodded miserably.

Atheleys let out a little sigh and stroked Eleanor's hair. "Perhaps it will not be as bad as you fear."

"It could be worse," Eleanor mumbled.

"But you're not of my kind," Atheleys continued. "What I mean is, you can't stay out in the moors forever."

"I have to go back."

She nodded. "But I don't think you'll do anything you don't want to do. There's always a way. You've just not come to it yet."

"I must go back." Eleanor moved to stand up, but the strength in her legs almost failed her and she started to fall back. Atheleys pushed her up, and they stood together, looking out over the moorland. Slowly, arms linked, they walked through the heather and back to the path. Eleanor brushed her hair off her face as if to make herself look respectable. "I'll kill him," she decided. "There's nothing else to do. I'm going to go back there and kill the Hob. Thank you, Atheleys," she turned and hugged her friend. "I would not have survived without you. You will take care of him, won't you?"

Atheleys grinned. "Nothing but the best."

Eleanor was determined to kill Hobart Hurst, but upon returning to Pines Lodge she was shocked to discover that it would not be possible. For he was already dead.

Hobart Hurst, the man she had believed her father, and later considered a hobgoblin, had expired. He was slumped and ashen grey, propped up against the carved witch post in the kitchen, with Eleanor's hat pin sticking out of his eye. There were the beginnings of ugly bruises upon his face and his hair was matted and stuck at odd angles with dried blood. His legs flopped out at ninety degrees, his feet shod in only the very best of walking boots. The blood from Eleanor's premature birthing was still upon the flagstones, a stain of misery. The acrid scent of burnt soup loitered in the air – clearly no one had tended to the dish Eleanor had been preparing over twenty four hours ago. The fire had gone out.

Ellen Withers sat miserably at the kitchen table, holding a compress to the side of her bruised face. She rolled a hard little object over and over on the table top, an object that proved to be a molar tooth. She looked up as Eleanor stepped into the kitchen, and gave out a little sob. "You're not a ghost are you?"

Eleanor looked a state. Her skirts were caked in blood and earth from the moors. The shoulder of her tunic was ripped, her hair was in tatters as if she had been crawling through heather for hours. She looked pale, aside from the angry bruise around her eye. There was dried blood crusted around her nostrils, grime on her face, and clean streaks washed on her skin where the tears had fallen.

"I'm not dead," she whispered hoarsely.

"Oh, my sweet girl," Ellen sobbed. "What's happened with you and..."

"He's dead." Eleanor's voice wobbled. "He was born too early. He never stood a chance. I buried him out in the moors. I would have him nowhere near this house." She felt the tears start to pour again. She reached out an arm and pointed at Hobart, needing to focus on something else. Her revenge had been taken from her. "What happened?"

Ellen was staring down at the tooth. "He hit me so hard, it just popped out. Just like that."

"So you killed him?"

Ellen looked miserably across at the corpse of Hobart Hurst and shook her head. "I wish I could say I did, but that isn't my work."

"Who did it?"

"Who can say," Ellen sighed. "I'm not one full of learning, and I wouldn't like to say which strike was the deadly one. But between the two of them they made sure he wouldn't live another day. He might have survived had he not been so proud of what he'd done to you. Jeering about kicking the babe out of your belly..."

"Which two?"

"Your mother stuck that pin in his eye at the end. He'd probably have died anyway, but I suppose it'll have pierced his brain." Ellen looked up at her. "He was so angry when he heard about what had happened to you. And Mr Hurst there, jeering at him and saying it was all you deserved. Mr Hurst has always been strong and he's always been a bully, but he's getting old and he's no match for a young man's fury."

"Angus," Eleanor whispered, as the drover appeared at the back of the kitchen. He'd been outside in the yard, and heard their voices. He looked shaken, and probably hadn't slept the night previous. He took in Eleanor's appearance, and felt that he might fall apart. If he hadn't been delayed along the road he would have arrived here a few days early and all of this could have been avoided.

"Eleanor, I had no idea," he began, moving towards her as if to embrace her.

"You," Eleanor started. She darted for the table and snatched at the first thing she reached, a plate, and threw it at him. He ducked and the plate smashed against the wall.

"Eleanor!" Ellen shrieked. "That's our best crockery."

"It's true, isn't it? You're a married man. A single man can't get his drover's licence. You lied to me."

"I never actually said I wasn't married..."

Ellen screamed as a couple of tea cups went the same way as the plate.

"You lied to me," Eleanor sobbed. "You had me believe you loved me and you'd come for me. Now look at the unhappy mess you find. Our son is dead and buried on the moors, and I am beaten and broke."

Cautiously hurrying around the chasm between them, mindful that Ellen Withers had reached out to move the last of the crockery from Eleanor's range, Angus caught her before she dropped to the floor to be lost in misery by the body of her dead, murdered father. "Those were not lies. I never lied to you. I was coming back for you. I'm only so sorry I didn't come a few days earlier."

"But you have a wife."

Ellen put her tooth in her pocket and stood up from the table. "I'll go see to Maud," she said, and left the room.

Angus manoeuvred himself and Eleanor to the wide rocking chair by the window, and dropped into it, letting her curl up on his lap. He cradled her, resting his chin on her messy hair as she cried into his shirt. This whole sorry mess could be worked back to his uncle, if he was inclined to see things in that light. "I've been married almost a year now," he admitted. "And there's not a day when I don't regret being persuaded into such folly. I had my property and my age, but I had fanciful hopes of coming down here this year and finding you. But my uncle wanted me to get the licence and there was a local lassie all willing to get hitched. It was so easy and I wasn't sure that you'd have me. You've become a woman of the world; all these things you were telling me about in your letters. The people you were meeting. Estonians and Russians even, can you imagine it. I thought what is she going to want with a drover like me."

Eleanor gave him a tired thump into his shoulder and smiled into his neck. Bittersweet.

"It was too easy and I needed the licence. We were married and a few weeks later I was away again on the droving road. I've not seen her since."

"Do you love her?"

He laughed out loud. It felt strange to laugh, surrounded by so much misery. "No. It was a marriage of convenience for both of us. I needed my licence and she wanted to get away from her parents." He stroked her hair. "I was coming for you. I asked after you in the village and they sent me up here. When I got here there was screaming coming from the house, I didn't know what I was walking into. I just walked right in, and there he was beating your mother. He stopped when he saw me, and asked me what my business was. I spoke and I suppose they all realised quickly who I was. He was laughing, said he'd kicked it out of your belly and sent you off onto the moors to die. I just lost control, attacked the man." He looked down at his bruised knuckles. "I hit him straight on and he fell back at an angle; hit his head and we all heard this terrible crack. He just went slack, like the life had left him, and he dropped to the floor." He paused. It was over now. "I didn't know there was a child coming. I'm so sorry, Eleanor."

She squeezed her eyes shut. What good was talking? It was all lost. "Perhaps it was for the best. What would you have done anyway? We couldn't have married. I don't know what would have become of me. And even now, after everything, we still can't..." She felt him press her to him.

"None of it matters now. I'll hang for what I've done."

It was then that Eleanor remembered the cold body of Hobart Hurst.

"I don't see that you have to."

They looked up to see Ellen Withers and Maud hovering at the side of the room. Each woman sported bruises on their faces.

"I don't see how I can't. I killed the man. We could plead a defence for what he did to Eleanor, but I'm married to another, and it would only destroy Eleanor to drag her through the court like that."

"That's not what I mean." Ellen led the gently crying Maud to the table. She seemed to be the only collected person present. Angus was being far too honest in his dealings, as if Hobart Hurst deserved justice. "There's only us four that know what happened. I say we bury him, and keep quiet. Folk in the village hadn't cottoned on that Eleanor was with child. We'll tell Gillian she lost it and is heartbroken. I know Gillian's bitter but she won't tell anyone. You won't have to live with the shame of being an unmarried mother, and you won't hang for his death."

"But my husband is dead," Maud sobbed.

"Yes, and look at us," Ellen snapped back. "Look at us all. A merry bunch of bruises we make. All the bullying and the beatings we've taken over the years. And you just look at my leg. He crippled me. He was a bastard and I'm not sorry he's dead."

"People will know he's dead."

"No one knows but us." Ellen cupped her hands around Maud's frail fingers. "Come on, Mistress. I think we all deserve a bit of good fortune after what's gone on the past two days. I say this is what we do." She looked around the kitchen. No one looked offended by the idea of her suggested complicity in the crime. "We carry on as normal, no, as normal, I say," she hushed Maud. "Folks saw him in the village yesterday, so we won't deny he came here. Only that he set off early this morning, as he does, off on business. We don't know when he'll be back. Eleanor can stay here till she's fully recovered, then she can go back to Whitby, to keep her ear to the ground, like." She caught Eleanor's eye. "And there's no Hobart Hurst forcing you to marry anyone now. I say we all carry on as normal, and pretend he went off onto the moors on one of his business trips. People will eventually start asking questions, and then we can be just as surprised as the rest of them. It'll be months, believe me. Him away from here six months or more is nothing unusual, now, is it?"

The kitchen fell silent as they considered what Ellen put before them. Angus shifted in the rocking chair. Eleanor sat up a little straighter. Maud's hands stopped shaking. Angus looked across the women. "This could work."

"Of course it can," Ellen sounded put out, as if it were a surprise her idea had potential.

"Yes," Eleanor agreed. "I'll not see you hang for him."

"I could write Amos," Maud said.

"No," Ellen warned. "We're pretending Hurst is alive. Everything has to continue as normal. Look, we've got a couple of days before Mr Hodgkin is back from the mart. That's enough time to get this sorry state cleared up, the worst of our cuts and bruises tidied up. Dresses washed and patched. I'll clean up the kitchen here, scrub down the floors. You three take him out onto the moors and bury him. But find a good place. Don't want Mr Hodgkin finding a freshly dug grave whilst he's out walking the property."

"The mound," Eleanor whispered, thinking of the abandoned hob mound Atheleys had talked of. There would be a certain justice in planting that wicked old man in an old hob hole. "There's a mound out on the moors. There's a cairn on it. We could take down the stones, dig a hole and bury him, then put the stones back. Mr Hodgkin would never notice."

"Rocks would keep foxes and the like from digging him up," Ellen concurred. "Maud, Eleanor, you go fetch the shovels from the barn. I'll go fetch an old sheet to roll him up in. Mr MacCaskill can carry him up there, strapping young lad like yourself. It's dark now, best head off as soon as possible so you won't be seen."

"You won't come with us?" Angus asked.

Ellen shook her head and stuck her deformed ankle out from the bottom of her dress. "He did that to me. I don't walk too good; I'd only hold you up. I'll hold the fort here and get the place cleaned up. Don't want anyone walking in by accident and seeing a pool of blood."

Eleanor jumped to her feet, feeling surprisingly energised despite everything that had passed the last two days. "Let's get this done. Mama," she held out her hand. "Let's fetch the shovels."

Ellen Withers proved herself to be a level headed task master. She soon had the hat pin extracted from Hobart's eye socket (no need leaving any evidence with the body, she said) and Hobart rolled up like a parcel and awaiting delivery. Water was on the boil for the cleaning task at hand. Broken crockery was swept up, knocked furniture righted. By the time dawn came the house would look as though no horror had ever happened. She gathered up the Hob's coat, walking stick and satchel and gave them to Eleanor to carry to the grave site. Maud took the shovels and Angus carried the body.

Eleanor led the way through the dark, down the winding sheep track to the little bubbling beck, over the waters and up the hill at the other side to the ascending moorland beyond. They walked in single file in silence, eager to be done with their work. At the mound the three worked at pulling the cairn apart, and as soon as the ground at the centre was visible, they started to dig. Eleanor and Maud took turns with one of the shovels, whilst Angus took on the major share of the work. His overcoat and waistcoat were tossed to the heather as the sweat built up, sticking his shirt to his back.

Dawn was breaking as the three stood at the rough hole, peering into the peaty dank depths. It was enough. They rolled Hobart Hurst into his final resting place, throwing his belongings in after as grave goods, then started to shovel the earth back in. Angus would habitually hop down into the hole to compress the earth down, so that there wouldn't be too much of a mound left, although it did look at certain angles as though he danced upon the grave. With the earth back in place, they started on rebuilding the cairn. As the sun rose in the sky to send the first rays down the valley, the final rocks were replaced, and the Hob was finally buried.

"Hob's Cross," Eleanor muttered as they stood in a line, paying their begrudging respects to a hard little man. "That's what we should call this place."

"He was not all bad," Maud said quietly. She met Eleanor and Angus's horrified stares. "What he did was unforgiveable. But he saved me once. I can't forget that."

"He wasn't really my father?"

Maud shook her head. "I carried you before he asked me to marry him. I know the terror of the unmarried mother, but he chose to save me. I was just a maid in a house and I made a mistake." She broke off, thinking back to where she had come from, a little village in the rolling hills of West Riding. "He brought me here for a fresh start, and then you and Gillian were born."

"Stephen's not his child either, is he?"

Maud shook her head.

"But Clara..."

"Clara is his full blood daughter. But she can never know, she and Stephen must never know the truth."

"Of course." Eleanor looked to the grave site, wondering if she dared ask, and if she did ask, if she would get an answer. "Who is my father?"

Maud smiled sadly. "A man I once loved." She walked over and picked up the two shovels. "I'll take these back to the barn before they're missed."

Eleanor watched her mother retreat from the mound. She wondered if she would ever learn anymore of where she came from. She'd have to tackle her mother about it again, at another time, when this all was just a memory. They'd have to play the game for the following months, perhaps years, and then maybe at some point they could apply to the magistrate to have their missing father declared dead. If all went well.

"What will you do now?"

"I don't know," Eleanor said sadly. She wiped at her eyes with the back of her hands. "Get better. Then do what Ellen says. Act as normal. Back to Whitby."

"Will you marry that man?"

She heard the jealously in his voice. She would rather be an old maid than marry Gerard Gaskin, and now that the Hob was gone, she would play the game and stay out of the Gaskins' grasp. "No," she looked over at her man. Her married man. "But this is the end, isn't it? You have your wife in Scotland."

He took her hand. "I'd like to think of this as a new beginning. As the start of many things."

She squeezed his fingers.

"It's not over. This is only just the start."

A Note Upon Hobgoblins

Hobgoblins are an old folk belief from, but not exclusively of England. The belief in the little folk appears all over Europe under one name or another, be it hobgoblin, goblin, troll, trowie, elf, fairy or whatever name they prefer to go by at your local forest. Some could be helpful to human neighbours and do jobs for them. Some caused mischief and trouble. Some could be heard playing the fiddle late at night. Some were even known to steal human babies.

Whilst this is a work of fiction, and whether hobgoblins did or do exist I will leave for you to decide, there are a number of folkloric inspirations that feature in this book. The only one who can proclaim complete creation by the author is in fact Atheleys. Having said that, the keen walker on the moors above Commondale can find old hob mounds/cairns, complete with markers. I will make no attempt to suggest who may have lived there.

In the Peak District, on the moorland above Chatsworth there is a small, square prehistoric burial mound that will be of no interest to most of the population aside from strange folk like myself who love a good Stone Age arrangement. What is relevant about this burial site is its later folkloric name, Hob Hurst's House. It was named after the hobgoblin that was reputed to live there at one time (and I hope he had a roof on the house at the time for the rain on the moors can be unforgiving). Hob Hurst, also known as Hob Thrush as the stories go, was known to help out a local shoemaker with a bit of cobbling.

In the Esk Valley, North Yorkshire, the River Esk works its way through the moorland down towards the coast and its entrance to the sea at Whitby. Here there are also tales of hobgoblins, some of which are referred to during this story. In Glaisdale, on the route along the River Esk, there was a hob of Hart Hall who would dress in a ragged shirt and flail (threshing by hand with a flail) at night for a local farmer.

A Note Upon The Book

This is a work of fiction. Whilst I have attempted to create the landscape and the history of the time, it will undoubtedly be crawling with errors and inaccuracy.
Most of the characters are completely fictional and products of the author's imagination. Any character (and for this book I mean only Mary Harker) who did exist in life appears here as a highly fictionalised version of themselves.

Please heed Angus' final words: It's not over. This is only just the start.